DESTINED
FOR HELL

DESTINED FOR HELL

Luis Torres
With
Kim Mailes

FIRST PRINTING, August 1985
SECOND PRINTING, February 1986

Typesetting by SPACE
(Sharp Printing & Computer Enterprise)
Berryville, AR 72616

Library of Congress Number: 85-062007
ISBN Number: 0-89221-133-4

Contents

Foreword 7

Chapter 1. The Skinny Man 11

Chapter 2. The Rejected Boy....................... 17

Chapter 3. The Big Apple........................... 21

Chapter 4. The Mystery Lady...................... 27

Chapter 5. Hello Mom.............................. 37

Chapter 6. The Shooting Gallery................... 45

Chapter 7. Down, Down, Down.................... 53

Chapter 8. Life of Crime........................... 61

Chapter 9. Mom Knows............................ 67

Chapter 10. Maria 75

Chapter 11. My Big Surprise 83

Chapter 12. I need A Fix 89

Chapter 13. Jesus 95

Chapter 14. I Found Him 103

Chapter 15. A Changed Life 107

Chapter 16. Free At Last 117

Epilogue 125

DEDICATION

To my precious
wife and helpmate
Gail

Write Luis at:
Luis Torres
Post Box 556
Sapulpa, OK 74067

Luis Getting ready to preach the Word

FOREWORD

The life story of Luis Torres is a miraculous event that is constantly happening in our society and many times we don't see it. DESTINED FOR HELL is the story of a man who experienced all the misfortunes in life. Luis Torres started as a loser, product of a broken family caught up in witchcraft, a cocoon of despair and hopelessness. It was true that he was DESTINED FOR HELL unless there was divine intervention of a powerful, loving God.

It was very obvious that God, Himself, through Jesus Christ, with strong holy hands pulled him out from the rat hole of life which is the lowest a human being can go, into the most powerful, glorious experience of relationship with Jesus Christ and gave him a glimpse into the heaven that lies ahead.

This book will make you laugh and cry, angry and glad, and you will feel the pain of his growth. Luis has grown to a point of being an inspirational and dynamic speaker before crowds that hunger for the knowledge of God. We need more miraculous lives such as Luis Torres'.

You won't be able to put the book down. Fasten your seatbelt and let us begin the DESTINED-FOR-HELL journey of Luis Torres.

Nicky Cruz

Chapter One

The Skinny Man

"Luis Torres," the loudspeaker blared, "You have a visitor!"

Who would want to visit me? The announcement distracted my thoughts from the poker cards I held in my hand. Several of my fellow inmates peered at me from their bunks while the readers looked over the tops of their pulp novels and the card players laid their hands down. Visitors were rare in this cell block.

"Hey man," said the big black man across the table, "aren't you going to see who it is?"

"Yea, OK," I said, "I'm going." I rose slowly and shuffled toward the bars. I couldn't imagine who might visit me. What kind of person visits hopeless, strung-out Puerto Rican junkies?

It couldn't be my family, they had finally given up on me. They supported me longer than I had expected them to.

The visitor couldn't be one of my friends. My friends wouldn't dare come to a prison, most of them were fugitives.

Besides, I found my circle of friends a bit small when I was busted and out of dope. Huh! Friends? Those lousy guys were the ones that got me started on heroin. Oh well, I guess they weren't to blame, I practically begged them to introduce me to the snowy white drug.

I knew the visitor wasn't my court appointed attorney. He finally showed up last week, took one look at my case and pronounced it hopeless. WHO COULD IT BE?

I had been in prison before, but this time was by far the worst. I had always been able to post bond using some alias or skip out on parole. This time I faced fifteen to thirty years for armed robbery. The police had finally put the jigsaw puzzle pieces of my record together and I wasn't going to get off with a slap on the wrist. I probably wouldn't see daylight for a long, long time.

Handcuffed, I obediently followed the guard down the hallway toward the visiting room, head down, eyes dejected. I had finally been forced to face my hopelessness.

For the first time in five years I was free from the physical addiction of drugs. Several weeks in prison had cured my body's $100 a day heroin habit the hard way: cold turkey. No words can really describe the torment the body feels as the demon powder releases its last tentacle.

Time behind bars had freed my body, but nothing cured the addiction in my mind. I desperately craved one more shot of my killer. Those first few days without heroin were like being placed on Satan's torture rack.

Only someone who has undergone withdrawal from drugs really knows the horror of returning to the land of the living. The pain is indescribable as the flesh sweats out the last traces of its dearest friend and most deadly enemy. Frigid chills and harrowing heat flashes race simultaneously through the muscles. Teeth chatter and eyeballs feel as though they will pop out of the skull. Cramps pull skinny limbs into a fetal position and bones ache as though in a metal crusher.

But now I was free, if you call living in a corral with a herd of animals free. That's not living. I wanted out, but there was no escape. This time the long arm of the law had reached out and embraced me in an unloving hug. She wasn't about to let me slip from her grasp.

I had been convinced that I was the master of my madness. Finally I had to face the real master of my life, and I was not he. My family, my friends, now even the cocky guy I used to be had walked out on the junkie I really was. What friend could I possibly have left? Who would waste their time coming to see a man destined for hell?

Led by the guard like a dog on a leash, I finally entered the small visiting center. Yawning, the guard pointed to the lone stranger in the corner. With two giant strides of the legs inside the 38" inseams he was across the room, hand outstretched, face sliced into a wide grin.

"Hello, Luis," he said, "I'm Jay Cole." For what seemed like minutes I stared at the outstretched right hand. Finally my eyes traced it up, up, and up, into the face of this beanstalk of a man. Who in the world is this guy? The skinny fellow created a most unusual picture with his worn, black, polyester suit, skinny black tie, big black Book, and boyish grin. I almost laughed, this guy looked like he had just left a masquerade party. It wasn't that he was poorly dressed or anything, he just looked like he had stepped out of one of those late-night black and white movies.

Eventually what manners I had left prevailed and I feebly shook the outstretched hand, my handcuffed left arm involuntarily responding. As he enthusiastically pumped my right hand, the chain between it and the left jingled like sleigh bells. We sat down, facing each other across one of those visiting tables you see in old Perry Mason reruns.

"I'm Jay Cole and I represent a rehabilitation program called Teen Challenge," he said. "Luis, God can help you. He helped Danny Santaluccia and he can help you."

Yea sure. I've been through all of this stuff before. I've been in every rehabilitation program in the Delaware Valley, nothing works for me. Besides, what do I care about some guy named Danny?

"Danny was in trouble just like you," he continued. "He

13

was hooked on drugs, facing prison time, hopeless. He asked Christ into his heart and now he's doing great. God will do the same thing for you if you'll just ask Him."

I may have been down for the count, but I wasn't out. It was OK for me to realize how desperate I was, but no one else was going to say I was hopeless. Though visitors here were few and far between, I was really getting fed up with this religious fanatic and I wanted him to leave. The old street-cool began to boil, and it soon frothed over the top of my calm exterior. I tossed my head back, cigarette held at a jaunty angle, smoke curling around my head.

As I began to speak, the smoke shot past the toothpick held in my mouth in short, staccato blasts. "Mister," I said, "I'm sure your Teen Challenge program is great for guys that are really messed up, but I'm OK. They're going to let me out of here, and when they do, I don't need you or your stinkin' program to get my act together."

Not a word was true; he and I both knew it. But, the street-wise kid in me wasn't about to let this funny-looking guy make a fanatic out of me. I hadn't lived on the streets all this time for nothing. No preacher was going to change me.

"OK, OK," he said. "Just let me pray for you before I go."

"Fine," I shot back, "go ahead and pray." I thought this would satisfy him and he would leave. I failed to realize he was a Pentecostal preacher. Both of us stood to our feet, and the skinny giant before me placed both hands on the top of my head and began to pray.

"Oh, God, SAVE HIM!" he cried. Why, with the opening of his prayer he nearly scared the devil out of me! The prayer grew louder as it continued, and did it continue! It lasted forever, sometimes even slipping into some foreign tongue. I looked through Jay Cole's long fingers into the eyes of the guard, and I could tell he and I were thinking the same thing, THIS GUY'S NOT WRAPPED TOO TIGHT!

"God, make Yourself real to him," he prayed. "Let him know that You can change his life. I rebuke you, Satan, in the Name of Jesus! Loose him from the bondage of mainlining. Set him free today!"

He finally finished praying. I had gone to religious education classes as a boy, but I had never heard anything like this. As he opened his eyes, I noticed tears spilling from them. Slowly, he reached for his handkerchief and mopped up the tears. Handing me some gospel tracts and his telephone number, he told me to call him as soon as I was released. Mister, I thought, you will wait a long, long time.

Saying he would pray for me, he was gone. The guard and I retraced our steps and once again I was "home." He released me from the handcuffs and shoved me inside, the bars banging shut behind me.

"Hey, Torres," shouted one of the guys, "you get religion?"

"Yea," called another, "we heard your priest praying clear in here. He gonna get you out?"

I stood with my back to them for several moments, staring through the bars at freedom. As Jay Cole walked away, I had a profound feeling sweep over me, an awesomeness hard to explain. I had met a powerful new force and I didn't know how to feel. The taunts continued in the background and I finally spun around to face the hecklers, voice filled with anger.

"Lay off!" I shouted. I walked to my bunk and threw myself into its lumps. Jay Cole was weird, really out in left field. But why did his prayer bother me so much? Maybe I really was hopeless. Maybe that social worker that just shook her head and left last week was right. Maybe I was too far gone.

Idly, I picked up one of the gospel tracts he had given me and began to read. It was called *"Don't Meth' Around"* and it talked about that "Danny" guy. The tract talked about the mess he was in before he got religion. "Wow," I muttered under my breath, "that guy was really messed up." Then suddenly it hit me, I WAS AS BAD AS THIS GUY I CONSIDERED ALL MESSED UP!

Angrily I wadded the tract into a ball and threw it across

the room. Rising from the bunk I called to the poker players, "Hey, man, deal me in." But agony throbbed through my mind as I walked across the room. Where had I gone wrong? Why had my world collapsed? What ever happened to the innocent child from Puerto Rico?

God can take a Nobody, and make him a Somebody, then he can go out and tell Everybody about Somebody who can change Anybody

Chapter Two

The Rejected Boy

I was born in the warm sunshine of Ponce, Puerto Rico, in 1950. Problems don't bother a boy who plays barefoot in the sand.

My grandfather was one of the most respected citizens of Ponce, serving as the chief of police for many years. He was a big, robust man. Grandfather had a big mustache and his sharp eyes could bore holes in the mightiest of men. In spite of his toughness, he was an extremely gentle man around his family. I can remember crawling up into his big lap in the warm tropical breezes of evening to hear the wonderful stories he would tell. My family says that I remind them very much of him. I received my height from him. Though I am not an exceptionally tall man, I am much taller than anyone else in my family. I count it an honor to be compared to him, he was quite a man.

The problems in my life stemmed largely from the divorce of my parents. Though I was a happy child at the time, it would not be many years before the impact of divorce hit me. I was fifteen years old before I met my mother. I did not know what she looked like or where she lived. Most of all, I did not understand why I couldn't live with her. Soon after my birth she moved to New York City, taking my two older sisters, Nettie and Alma. Mom and Papi, (these are the family names for my mother and father), had separated before I came along. I was the youngest of four children born to their marriage. My sister Nettie is 6 years older than I am, my sister Alma is 3 years older, and my only brother Willie (called Junior by the family) is 2 years my senior. I am told my parents' marriage was never very good, and by the time I was born they had separated. My mother left as soon after my birth as she as able. The first four years of my life were spent in the custody of my grandparents.

My father's family was against my parents' marriage from the beginning. They felt Papi was worthy of a better wife. Though not wealthy, the Torres family was well respected in Ponce, and my mother was beneath them in the social structure.

A great conspiracy surrounded my birth because of the family's antagonism. About the time I was conceived my father was seeing a woman named Luisa, who later became my stepmother. My father's family approved of Luisa and in later years contended that I was really her child rather than Mom's.

The unspoken and unseen rivalry between Mom and Luisa lasted for many years. Luisa was very involved in spiritism; in fact, many came to her to ask her to cast spells on their enemies. Many in my family say that Luisa put a curse on Mom that caused the problem. This situation was made even more confusing by the fact that Mom and Luisa had been best friends for many years. They had played together as children and had remained friends through their teenage years. I am sure that there are many parts of the story that remain untold to this day.

Due to the strong Catholic influence on the Puerto Rican people, divorces were extremely difficult to obtain on the island. Because he could secure a divorce more easily in the United States, Papi moved to New York with Luisa a few months after I was born. My father was an intelligent and hardworking man, so he had little difficulty finding work in New York. He immediately became a delivery truck driver for a toy manufacturing company in Manhatten. Luisa found work in the same company. They still work faithfully for the same firm. It was not until several years after their arrival in New York that a divorce was obtained, and they legally became husband and wife.

Thousands of Puerto Ricans made their way to new homes in New York during the early 1950's because of better jobs. Members of the family already settled in New York were a great help to Papi and Luisa. But in a way, they never really left Puerto Rico. All of my life I have heard Puerto Rican people speak fondly of home. Many return to Puerto Rico often, some doing without luxuries so their often small income will cover the expense. The lure of home pulls strongly on the Latin people.

Looking back, I suppose the lack of a mother was the major reason my life took such a desperate turn. I did not realize it at the time. I was just a happy boy playing in Puerto Rico. Living without a mother and father for the first four years of my life and living without a mother for another twelve years did me great harm. It wasn't simply the absence of a mother that was so hard for me to understand. Many children grow up without a mother so my case was not so unusual in that respect. But the nagging question that continually haunted me was; why?

The child of most divorced homes lives with one parent and knows the reason is because mom and daddy can't get along. All of my growing up years I was haunted by the knowledge that neither parent really wanted me. Papi provided a good home, but it seemed to me that Luisa resented me. The greatest hurt of all was not knowing my mother.

I lived pleasantly in Puerto Rico until my father called for me to join him in New York. I recall very vividly the day I left Puerto Rico for my new home in New York City. I was four years old and the big silver plane that would carry me to the United States fascinated me. The temperature in San Juan was a balmy 85 degrees; the warm ocean breeze blew through my coal-black hair, and the familiar faces of my aunts smiled around me. Their love was the only love I had known. Though I was leaving everything familiar, I had no fear and skipped happily to the plane in the new black-patent shoes purchased especially for the trip. I raced joyfully up the stairs and disappeared into the plane, all my worldly possessions tied in the shoe box slung over my shoulder.

My life changed drastically the moment our plane landed at LaGuardia airport. I was tired and irritable, and my new shoes had proven far too small and were hurting my little feet. The thin cotton shirt I wore offered little protection from the blustery winds of New York. I finally stepped from the door of the plane onto the stairway, shoebox of possessions and too-tight shoes clutched in my hands. I was tired and cranky. Cocooned in a huge airline blanket some kind stewardess had wrapped around me, I stood in the cold. I scanned the people standing in the bleak and smoggy New York drizzle and finally found a small band of Puerto Rican strangers who surely were the ones who had come to meet me. I felt very alone.

Luis Speaks at a Womens Prison

Chapter Three

The Big Apple

My new family and I grinned awkwardly at one another for a few moments before hustling toward the late model station wagon in the parking lot. Only my sister Nettie lived with Papi and Luisa before I came to New York. The little family leaving La Guardia airport would soon begin to multiply, however. Papi and Luisa were about to begin their own family, and it wouldn't be long until Papi's station wagon was filled — to capacity.

Nettie had lived with Papi and Luisa since they moved to New York from Puerto Rico. Being an only child was not her idea of fun, and she was overjoyed to have her little brother around. I immediately became her giant baby-doll. Papi was happy to have his young son with him again, and Luisa seemed reconciled to the idea. It took our new family several months to become acquainted. Papi had not seen me since I was a babe in arms.

Although I was unaware at the time, Mom lived in another part of the city with my sister Alma. My parents had made arrangements for the custody of the children when they were divorced. Papi agreed to raise Willie and me, and Mom agreed to care for the two girls. Another part of the agreement was a secret. Mom had fallen in love with another man and was to be married. Her new husband was aware of Mom's former marriage and the girls, but he didn't know about Willie and me. Mom was afraid her new husband would leave if he knew she had four children, two of them unruly boys. Everyone involved agreed not to tell him about Willie and me. Of course, I had no trouble keeping the secret; I had no knowledge of Mom or her new husband. All I knew was that I was the son of some unknown mother.

My aunts in Ponce did not own a car, so I thought Papi must be very wealthy to afford such luxury. I soon discovered that Papi was far from wealthy, but he always had a station wagon to transport his growing family. Owning an automobile was very unusual in our neighborhood. Few of our neighbors could drive and none of them owned a car. Papi took great pride in his car and kept it in top notch condition. My family has always treated their possessions with care. Many of the families in our neighborhood allowed their houses to run down and were less than careful about their clothing and grooming, but not the Willie Torres, Sr. family. We may have been poor, but we were always clean and our meager possessions were always in good repair. Papi was proud of the fruits of his honest labor. I am grateful for that upbringing to this day.

I rode in silence, my too-small shoes and shoebox still clutched tightly in my arms. I considered Ponce a huge city, but I starred in wide-eyed fascination as we joined the endless stream of automobiles heading downtown. I couldn't believe there were this many people in the entire world, much less in one city. The silence began to break as we drove along, and soon my new family and I were chattering like old friends.

We worked our way between the skyscrapers and over the bridges until we finally arrived at my new home in the heart of the Bronx near Yankee Stadium. For the next few years my address would be 811 Tinton Avenue. My family never lived in the government project houses. I suppose the places we lived were what you would call ghettoes, but I did not know it until years later. When your entire world is poor, you are unaware of your poverty. We never lived in the worst of the ghettoes, however.

We referred to the place we lived as our "house," but it was really an apartment. The 811 Tinton Avenue apartment was typical of those in our neighborhood. The building was five stories tall and we lived on the third floor. Each apartment contained a living room, a kitchen, two bedrooms and a bath. Our apartments always had running water and Papi insisted our home be kept very clean.

We moved three times while I lived in New York with Papi, but never more than a few blocks from the old address. Excepting the times I rode in Papi's delivery truck, I was 16 years old before I left the ten square block area of our neighborhood. I can remember making toy doll deliveries in the big, ten-wheeled truck. I shifted the gears while he drove and pushed the big clutch pedal. I didn't see the Statue of Liberty until I was grown. Though we lived within a few blocks of Yankee Stadium, I never saw a ballgame.

We lived on Tinton Avenue for five years and then moved one-half block away to a larger apartment in a smaller building. We moved because of the growing size of the family, but also because of the increasing number of blacks in our neighborhood. Racial tension was a way of life in the Bronx. My world was mostly black and brown. Ricky Ricardo's wife Lucy was about the only white person I knew, and she entered our home through Papi's black and white television set. Everyone who lived in our neighborhood was either Puerto Rican or black. As always, there were good and bad people of both races and I had many black friends. I suppose some bigotry was involved in our moves, but Papi loved an all Puerto Rican neighborhood. Our last home in the Bronx was the Puerto Rican neighborhood of the seven hundred block of 158th Street.

The Hispanic neighborhood is a city unto itself. If I

closed my eyes, I could almost believe that 811 Tinton Avenue was Ponce. Everyone spoke Spanish and we knew suppertime was near when we smelled the familiar aroma of rice and beans escaping from Luisa's kitchen window. Our world was a continuous whirl of Spanish music, drinking, and spiritism.

Most Puerto Rican people are very devout Catholics. However, there are some who are not. As a result, many of them devote portions of their homes to images. Images are used many times to consult the dead or to place a curse on an enemy. Those who have power in the spirit world are often consulted by others. They are paid to contact the dead or to place a curse on an enemy.

My stepmother was very involved in the spirit world. A large closet in our house was maintained solely for spiritist activities. Providing food for the images was a daily ritual. As she placed each day's offering before the images, she removed the untouched fare from the day before. Luisa often performed rituals to please the spirits of the shrines.

Our neighbors, the Rojas family, devoted the largest room of their house to the images. Their son Celestino was my best friend. His parents were said to have great power and would perform spiritualism for a fee. One evening my family visited the Rojas home for a special event. Many of our neighbors were already seated around the room as we arrived. As we entered the home the eerie strains of spiritist music wafted its notes through the house. Spiritist music is a derivitive of voodoo music. The playing of this music helps the participants contact the spirit world. The most common spiritist song is *"The Lady Dressed in White."* The Lady Dressed in White is the patron saint of all spirits. She must be contacted before any spiritual activity can take place.

A funeral was the reason for the gathering and the body of a large Dominican man was the center of attention. Several participants were already praying around his dead body. Placing the embalmed body in the home of a spiritist is common. The man's family was willing to pay a large sum of money to make contact with the spirit and determine the fate of his soul.

As can be imagined, several hours spent in the company of a dead body and a host of chanting spiritists is an unsettling experience for a little boy. The eerie prayers continued into the wee hours of the morning. The mourners chanted liturgies over and over, desperately attempting to contact the Spirit world. The phonograph needle continued its scratchy path around *"The Lady Dressed in White"* and shadows from the shrine candles danced on the walls of the crowded apartment.

Suddenly, my oldest sister Nettie fell to the floor, controlled by the spirit of a snake. The chants and singing grew in intensity as she twisted and contorted into the satanically inspired image of a serpent. Hissing loudly, she slithered around the room as others quickly cleared a path. On her belly, she made her way under every piece of furniture in the house as she moved from room to room. No one present doubted the experience, many had been similarly possessed. Finally, she collapsed into an exhausted heap. The bestowal of such an experience was considered a great honor and all gathered around to congratulate her on being so favored.

The spiritist activities frightened me greatly at first. When attending the seances, I cowered in the corner, keeping my eyes shut as tightly as possible. But, it wasn't long until I felt comfortable around spiritism and was no longer afraid. The frightening activities of those dark nights was always followed by the brightness of a new day and life went on.

Soon I grew comfortable in my new neighborhood. I did not have many close friends but I liked everyone and everyone liked me. This was to be the pattern of my life. I was friendly and enjoyed the company of others, but I would never let anyone get too close. I suppose you could have called me a pleasant loner.

I entered school at age five, attending P.S. 24 two blocks from home. I was a very good student in elementary school and popular with the teachers. There were not many students who really cared about learning at P.S. 24.

Weekends and summer days were spent playing stickball in the streets or riding homemade go-carts down dead man's hill. I thought dead man's hill was terribly treacherous when I was a little boy, but it was really only a small incline. Life was pretty good in those days; we had plenty to eat and we thought we might be able to "get ahead" someday.

There was always something missing in my life though. I desperately wanted to know my mother. Children were born to Papi and Luisa, but they did not really seem like my brothers and sisters. I could tell Luisa did not like me. Looking back, I think the reason she took that attitude was because I was the son of her rival. Though she had stolen the husband of her best friend, Luisa always had a fear of losing Papi back to Mom.

I suppose Papi did his best to be a good father and, in many ways, he was. But Papi was never very good at showing his love and affection. After I came to New York and Nettie went back to Puerto Rico, I was very much alone. I desperately needed someone to tell me who I was and why I was alive. I can remember sitting on the stoop at night, staring up at the stars in the patch of sky between the buildings, wondering why no one loved me. I was only a little boy, but I knew there was a force beyond this world because of my familiarity with spiritist activities. I wondered who He was and where I fit into His plan.

On a hot day during the summer before I was to begin second grade, my father told me my brother Willie was moving to New York. I did not even know Willie but the news excited me; finally I would have a real brother! Along with Willie would come a baby girl Patti, who was being adopted by Papi and Luisa. Luisa had begun to suffer from depression, and it was felt that a little girl to go with all of the boys in the house would please her. Willie's coming had a positive effect on me immediately. Even though we had to become acquainted, there was a special bond between us. There was finally someone in our house I could identify with. Willie was to become very special to my life in the next few years. I entered school confidently that fall; my brother was coming with me!

Chapter Four

The Mystery Lady

Wow! Big brother is going to school with me!

Though Willie was just two years older, he seemed like a giant to me. Willie has always been built like a weight-lifter.

Ha, Ha! Those bullies won't chase me home from school anymore. I was often harassed because I was an easy target for the school hoodlums. When the final bell rang, I always slipped down the stairway and peered around the corner of the big, red-brick building, warily expecting the troublemakers. The older ruffians were often waiting and off to the races we went, me running as if for my life. Down Caldwell Avenue, around the corner candy store, across Tinton Avenue and up the stairs of our building I raced, lungs begging for air as the laughter of my pursuers cackled in my ears.

Willie understood that I just wasn't a fighter. I wasn't a coward, violence was just contrary to my personality. I was a thinker, a happy solitaire. Willie was the first to really understand. He protected me, telling my attackers to leave me alone, and they usually did as Willie Torres

27

said. Though he was the roughest character to hit our neighborhood, he never questioned my aversion to violence. He respected his unique little brother and I loved him for it.

Since he was grandfather's favorite, Willie was the last to leave Puerto Rico. If Willie hadn't been such a troublemaker, he would have remained in Puerto Rico. Willie was very headstrong, even as a child, always running with the rough-and-tumble crowd. Our ex-police chief Grandfather found Willie's constant troublemaking intolerable. The last straw came the day Willie broke Grandmother's cherished antique mirror while shadow boxing. He found himself on the next plane to New York, declared incorrigible at age 9. Everyone expected Willie to turn out bad, but never Luis. They were sure in for a surprise.

Willie immediately found friends in our rough neighborhood. Nine year olds were not old enough to join the street gangs but formed small auxiliaries called "the little people." In many ways the little people are far more dangerous than teenage gangs. The little people have no scruples, anyone or anything is fair game for their belligerent activity. Winning the respect of his teenage counterpart is the little person's highest goal, a goal for which he will pay any price. Being a gang member in the Bronx assured protection, but Willie made sure I was safe though uncommitted.

Willie and I complimented each other. I was always a loner, a thinker, and a part of me always wanted to be feared and respected like my brother. Willie was the exact opposite; an outgoing person, constantly surrounded by friends, unafraid, the center of the action. But Willie sometimes wished he could have been a little more like me. Our understanding was based on a special trust. We appreciated each other's uniqueness because a part of us wanted to be like his brother. Though I was perfectly capable of taking care of myself and was sometimes forced into doing so, I usually backed away from a fight with Willie's blessing. God help the boy who harmed Willie Torres's brother.

By the time Willie changed schools to Junior High School 38 on St. Ann's Avenue, I was well established in P.S. 24. My best friends in late elementary school and on into Junior High School were Celestino Coloso, a Puerto Rican, and Don Telly, a black. We spent a lot of time together and soon began to skip school frequently. Skipping school in my neighborhood was nothing unusual, it was very unusual for anyone to go to school more than half of the time. My parents worked from daylight until well past dark so they didn't know I was playing hooky. The teachers did their best, but we were hell-bent on becoming lifetime losers.

I did have one great ambition: to be a singer. I listened to the great Spanish singers for hours at a time. My idol was a crooner named Felipe' Rodriquez. I knew all of his songs by heart and imitated him as well as my pre-adolescent voice allowed. I sang constantly, the veins in my neck bulging as I strained to hit the high notes. I sang until the family cried, "Please, no more!" and then sang some more. I just knew the future would find me responding to the thunderous ovations of a jubilant crowd.

Celestino, Don, and I suddenly found girls more attractive, so we began spending a lot of time at the mirror. My friends nicknamed me "Anthony" because they said I looked like the movie star, Anthony Quinn. To this day, everyone in my old neighborhood calls me Anthony instead of Luis.

"Hey, Anthony," Don and Celestino would call. "Let's sing *There's a Moon Out Tonight!*"

We would huddle together, pulling our collars under our ducktail hairdos and harmonize. We stood on the street corners for hours, crooning for the small crowds that gathered. We became quite good as our repertoire of 50's pop and Spanish opera songs expanded. When it rained, we slipped into the marble hallways of apartment buildings where we thought our voices sounded really good as they ricocheted off the hard walls.

My singing also proved profitable. As the neighborhood gang waited outside, Willie and I would step into a corner

29

candy store to put on a performance. I would climb on top of a box and begin singing my heart out while the storekeeper and his customers gathered around. Willie wore Papi's old coat with holes in the lining. While I sang Willie stuffed candy and cupcakes through the holes and into the lining. When the performance ended, everyone would applaud while the manager rewarded me with a piece of candy. Little did he know Willie was already out the door enjoying the ill-gotten gain.

Papi was too poor to give us an allowance so we carried groceries in return for tips. The neighborhood boys lined up outside Fedco Foods and waited for women with several heavy sacks of groceries to beckon for help. The small tippers soon learned to either be more generous or carry their own bags home. A gangster scorned is rather disagreeable.

The only seriously evil incident of my childhood came while I was carrying groceries. An older lady had purchased enough groceries to need two boys, so my friend Jose' assisted me. After seeing the inside of her apartment, Jose' and I decided she had to be wealthy. She gave us a very small tip, so we decided to rob her.

We waited at the door of her building until she finally emerged. I grabbed her purse and we hurried from the scene of the crime. The lady began screaming bloody murder behind us, doing her best to draw attention. As luck would have it, two police officers were just around the corner. They quickly caught up with us, and we knew that we were in serious danger of being arrested. The chase resembled a scene from the Keystone Cops as we tossed the purse back and forth, zigzagging through the traffic.

It didn't take us long to decide we would rather stay free than have the purse, so I threw it over my shoulder, hoping they would give up the chase. One of the policemen stopped to pick it up, but the other continued his pursuit. I yelled for Jose' to take a different route, and when we split, the policeman decided to follow me. Leaping as high as I could, I grabbed the bottom step of a fire escape and scampered up. When I reached the roof, I was completely winded and hid behind a smokestack, holding my breath. I hadn't prayed in years, but I remember thinking, "God, don't let that policeman see me!" He finally reached the roof but failed to see me and gave up. I decided right there that a life of crime was not for me.

Doing wrong was always easier than doing right. Every influence was evil. Willie was now thirteen years old and ready to become a full-fledged gang member. Almost every young man in the neighborhood was a member of the gang. Those who did not belong to the gang were either sissies whose fear of the gangs kept them indoors or had an alibi like me. My alibi was Willie. Even though Willie was the youngest of the gang members, his tough reputation allowed his little brother to remain independent.

Even girls belonged to gangs. They formed auxiliaries to supply the guys with sex. Teen gang members are the worst male chauvinists on earth. Women are thought of as objects to provide sex. It is no wonder the girls, "dolls" in street vernacular, are vain and jealous. They compete ruthlessly to be the girlfriend of the most violent boys.

Our neighborhood gang was known as the "Christian Knights" and was made up of those in the Caldwell Avenue "turf." Willie was admired by the older boys because of his reckless daring and willingness to fight. The gangs had an elaborate system which rewarded the most outstanding with leadership positions. It wasn't long until Willie had worked his way up the ladder to become war counselor. Willie was the smallest member of the gang, but the most ruthless.

The war counselor is the most important leader of the gang except for the president. Being war counselor is sometimes more powerful than being president because he arranges all gang wars, and gang wars are the biggest reason the gang exists. Willie loved to fight too much to become president of the gang. The president does not fight; he simply directs the battle.

A gang war is the worst fear of any neighborhood. There were many gangs in the Bronx, and the sound of gunfire and sirens can be heard almost every night. All sorts of dangerous weapons are used in these battles. A few carried some sort of firearm, but used switchblades or garrison belts. These teenagers are expert killers and can slice a man to pieces in a moment with a switchblade knife or bash in a skull with a garrison belt. Some of the gang members used zip guns that were almost as dangerous to them as the target. Zip guns are broken automobile antennaes fitted with screen-door hardware to fire .22 caliber bullets.

One of the most brutal gang wars in history took place right in front of our house when I was about ten years old. Two of the local gangs had been feuding all summer, and everyone knew that a major battle was coming. I hid under Papi's station wagon as the war rumbled down Tinton Avenue. The violence and blood were sickening, but worst of all was the killing of a baby boy. As the fighting raged, an eighteen month old Puerto Rican baby ran crying into the street. Inadvertantly, the bullet of a zip gun cut the infant down as he ran. The battle grew silent for a moment when they saw what they had done, but within seconds, it continued its bloody way down the street.

I just didn't like violence. I wanted to make peace, not war. Even today, the family turns to little "Luis" to be the peacemaker. The only time I can remember becoming violent was when Willie and I came to the table still arguing over a stickball game. Mealtime at the Torres household was a time of silence, so our disagreement had to be put on hold. So, when Papi wasn't looking, I threw my fork at my brother. Willie saw it coming and ducked, narrowly averting being skewered. The window behind him was not so lucky and shattered with a resounding crash. Willie still laughs about the only time I showed any fire.

I also thought about becoming a doctor. Healing sick people appealed to me. I never made the connection between good grades and medical school though. I was too busy playing hooky with my friends.

The applause of a crowded concert hall or the gratitude of someone healed would have given me great joy. I had a deep need for love and approval. I would do almost anything to make a friend. Consequently, others often took advantage of me, but I didn't mind if I could make someone happy. Sure, I was hard to get along with sometimes, but I found my pleasure pleasing others.

Some of the way I am is hereditary (My family says I am a carbon copy of my Grandfather.), but I know much of my craving for approval came because I rarely received any. Papi worked too hard to have time for his little boy, and Luisa had absolutely no use for me. My stepbrothers and stepsisters were a plague rather than a blessing. By this time Willie and I had three stepbrothers, one stepsister, and an adopted sister. If there was a family fight Luisa always took their side. Willie and I began spending every waking moment on the streets, the only place we were really welcome.

Our home wasn't happy, it was splintered in too many different directions. Papi's drinking and Luisa's nagging only grew worse as the years went by. Mealtimes were times of silence in our Puerto Rican home. This custom came from the unhealthy mix of family problems, personal problems, and stifling Hispanic customs. Our meals were eaten in silence broken only by snippets of conversation between Papi and Luisa. Mealtime became an exercise to fill our bellies rather than a time of family fellowship.

As my sixth grade year began to draw to a close Willie began to talk more and more about his future. He was obviously going nowhere, and he began to think seriously about the rest of his life. Willie had loved the sea from the time he was a little boy in Puerto Rico. This love, along with his fierce, independent spirit made the maritime a logical career choice. The public school system of New York includes a high school strictly for the training of young men who want to pursue a career in the merchant marines. In his last year of junior high school, Willie applied for admission to Maritime High and was accepted.

I stayed especially close to Willie that summer. Willie had been my strength since he came to New York, and I didn't want to see him leave. Life had been almost unbearable before he came, and I knew it would be worse when he was gone. Luisa and her children continually took sides against me. The coming of my brother had changed that. The others were still treated as favorites but now it was them against us instead of them against me. It would once again be me against the world when Willie went to sea.

We spent most of our time on the playgrounds that last summer. A middle-aged lady was very friendly to Willie and me all through June. Every day she called us to the wire mesh fence surrounding the basketball court to talk. She was a very nice lady, and I began to look forward to seeing her every day. She never said much, just smiled and asked how we were. She always gave us a treat, either a candy bar or a piece of fruit. I had no idea who our "mystery lady" was, and if Willie knew, he wasn't telling.

On a particularly hot day in August the friendly lady didn't come. The gang finally broke up as darkness fell over the Bronx, and Willie and I started home. As we bounced the basketball between us down the street, I said, "I wonder where the nice lady was today?"

"I don't know," Willie said. "Maybe she's not coming back."

"What makes you say that?" I asked.

"Oh, I don't know. I've just got a feeling she won't be back."

"I sure do like that lady, she's really nice."

"Yea," Willie replied. "You ought to like her."

"Sure I like her, she's a nice lady."

"No, I mean you should really like her a lot."

"What'cha gettin' at, Willie?" I knew my brother, something was up. I stopped under the street light on Caldwell Avenue and faced him.

"Well, you know when I was gone yesterday afternoon?" Willie said, bouncing the basketball on the sidewalk as it cast its long shadow down the street.

"Yea, I know," I replied. "C'mon, out with it."

"Well, I followed the nice lady to see where she went.

I've been doing a lot of thinking about that lady and I figured I knew who she was. I followed her back to a factory in Manhattan and waited across the street for her to get off work and then talked to her for a while."

Willie stopped and just stared out from under the shadow cast by the bill of his cap, batting the basketball back to earth as it sprang from the pavement. The night was still, as far as nights in the Bronx go. The wail of a siren floated on a distant breeze, a jazz band blared in the bar down the block, and the rhythmic "ping-ping" of the basketball continued.

"OK, man, cut the fun and games. I like that lady, who is she?"

"You should like her," Willie said. "She's your mother."

I fell against the telephone pole behind me, stunned. Willie started home, but I stood frozen. I stared at his back until he disappeared, watching until the dribble of the ball was just a silent motion. I slowly slid to the ground and hugged my knees, staining them with the hot tears that flowed down my cheeks.

Luis and Gail with the Pastor and students from the Rehab Program for men in Maranga, Brazil

Chapter Five

Hello Mom

Willie's dreams came true while mine fell apart. My brother left for Maritime High School in late August, and again, I was alone. Loneliness can live in a crowded apartment in the largest city in America. Though I had thousands of neighbors, I was isolated as though shipwrecked.

My position in the family was weakened instantly. No longer was I sure anyone would love me.

Papi wanted to provide the love and support I needed, but the bridge between father and son had long ago burned. I didn't resent Papi's attitude; he only did what he had to do. His first marriage had been a failure and he wanted this one to be different. I didn't understand Luisa's attitude. Maybe she was jealous of Papi's affection, maybe she was overprotective of her natural children. Whatever the reason, Luisa had no room in her heart for me.

To compound my troubles, I had met my mother, if you call accepting candy from a kind stranger meeting your mother. She was so near, yet so far away. I was better off ignorant. Now I knew she and I lived in the same city, but we might as well have lived on opposite sides of the globe. Why? My aching heart asked. Why?

Willie was expelled from Maritime High just before Christmas. He had been expelled for being a belligerent punk; and I guess he was.

Papi was furious. Willie's troublemaking had exhausted his patience. Maritime High had been his wayward son's last hope. When Willie blew it Papi said, "No mas!" Willie had worn out his New York welcome and soon found himself on a plane back to Puerto Rico. My brother was gone and disgraced.

My education continued at Bronxland Junior High School 38, and for the first time I began to notice the girls. Even more amazing, they began to notice me! My friends, Celestino and Don, became my substitute family. Our attendance and behavior was more delinquent than ever. We attended school every so often, but only to see the girls or to beat the heat when the Caldwell Avenue gangs were on the police wanted list.

Even though I still hated violence, I had defended myself several times when I had no choice and was now accepted. Everyone now knew I could fight if I had to, but I tried to avoid a confrontation. A few even began to admire my stand for peace and started asking me to settle disputes. Many gang members had been hurt or killed and a lot of the guys were wising up. Some still wanted to rumble, but the character of the neighborhood was changing.

Not everyone looked kindly on peacemakers though. Tommy McKnight was the gentle black giant of the neighborhood. His philosophy of peace and friendship was a lot like mine. Tommy was opposed by a bully named Charles Blake. When a smaller student accidentally got in Charles' way, he suffered the consequences. Tommy was a peacemaker, but seeing the bully pummel the little fellow exposed his violent nature. Tommy knocked Charles Blake into "never, never land" with one blow of his big fist. Following school, Charles' gang, the Rockets, was waiting. What they did to Tommy wasn't pretty, and it was some time before he was able to return to school. Sometimes it didn't pay to be a peacemaker in the Bronx.

The school year I had dreaded was turning out pretty good. I made friends with a lot of the guys and was having pretty good success with the girls too. But, when I was alone, I hurt worse than ever. I began to drink heavily to cover the pain. I didn't have any trouble finding reasons to drink, a life like mine was full of reasons. I drank when with my friends because they did. Then I drank when I was alone to forget they were gone.

At first, we got our liquor from our fathers' stock, but they soon became suspicious. Then we started buying cheap Gypsy Rose and Three Roses wine with tips from the Fedco customers. When our thirst became bigger than our earnings, we started burglarizing homes. A lot of the guys made money snatching purses, but an unpleasant memory kept me out of that scheme.

Most evenings found us on the street corners harmonizing. We dressed alike, trying to form an identity against the anonymous world around us. Our standard issue uniform included a bandero around the head, hair cut into a duck-tail, black leather jackets, pegged pants and pointed shoes. If the night was cold, a blazing barrel of trash warmed our outsides while we passed a bottle to warm our insides.

We were just children, but our criminal records were already becoming very impressive. Murder, rape, armed robbery, you name it, somebody in our gang had already become an expert. Sheer boredom caused some of our lawlessness. Most of the crimes were committed to support a drug habit. Nothing is more pathetic than a thirteen year-old junkie in withdrawal.

One thrill calls for another more stupendous. I was becoming an alcoholic, but I made it a point to stay away from drugs. I had been taught that drugs were bad news, and booze was enough high for me. Willie was the meanest fighter on the block, the most openly criminal, and the heaviest drinker, but he refused to mess around with drugs. "Drugs will kill you, Luis," he often told me. "Stay away from drugs."

The pain was too deep and my friends too persistent to hold out forever though. I remember very clearly the first time I smoked marijuana. Don Telly and I needed some money, so we spent the day scrounging for tips at the Fedco Food Store. The day's take wasn't very good, and we could only buy one bottle of the very cheapest wine. It was winter and the snow was piled in dirty mountains on the curb. We spent the early evening standing around a fire on the corner. The night was especially cold and lonely, and it was not long before our friends had passed the bottle around one time too many, and all it contained was the bottom.

As usual, the friends were gone with the liquor. One by one, they drifted off to some other haunt. When the fire died, Don and I took refuge in the entrance of an abandoned building.

"I sure wish we had the money to buy some more wine," I said, pulling my collar up against the cold.

"Here, try this," Don said, pulling a joint from the pocket of his leather jacket. "It's better anyway. Grass just gives you a real nice high, and no crash the next day either."

Willie's advice came to mind, but I decided there wasn't any harm in trying it. Besides, how could I be sure I didn't want the stuff unless I tried it? I took a deep drag on the rolled end of the short, white stick while Don cupped his hand around the lighter. I leaned back against the cold brick wall and felt a wonderful, euphoric feeling wash over me like a warm bath.

"You drag on it real deep, man, try another pull," Don said. I did as told and as I handed the joint to my friend I knew I had found paradise. There was none of the lost feeling of being drunk, just a peaceful obliviousness to the cruel world around me. I had graduated to upper division fantasy land. Willie was wrong, this was it.

I began to live for the sole purpose of getting high. I stopped going to school entirely, spending all of my time earning or stealing enough money for another bag of grass. I had been searching desperately for a better escape from boredom and this was it. Escaping boredom in the ghetto is a greater need than food or shelter.

Living where every corner is a circus sideshow shouldn't be boring, but boredom is the common denominator of the ghetto. Monotony stalks the ghetto-dweller as he drifts through the neighborhood haunts. Like a hunter running his traps, he makes the rounds, desperately searching for a relief from boredom. With lonesomeness tattooed across his face, he buys a beer in the neighborhood bar before sauntering out of its blackness. Pausing in the sunshine, he raps with his equally afflicted friends before shuffling on. Rounding the corner he buys a dream from his bookie in the back of the barbershop. Everyone is a gambler in the ghetto, wooing Lady Luck to take pity on them. Of course, betting is slow after the first of the month. The welfare check goes fast. When broke he stops by to see what could have happened "if only."

No one who grew up in the Caldwell Avenue neighborhood ever amounted to anything. My sister Alma had moved to Philadelphia to escape the inevitable dead end. She came to New York to visit our mother and stopped to see Papi. As usual, I wasn't home and she soon located me hanging out on the corner, drinking with some of my friends. She grabbed me by the ear and pulled me back home. My first reaction was embarrassment when my friends began to laugh. Only my big sister could get away with something like this! My next reaction was shock; it had been some time since anyone cared what I did. After giving me a real tongue-lashing, she invited me to come to Philadelphia to live with her. She knew I was going nowhere fast.

As dreadful as home was, I couldn't imagine living elsewhere. Though the ghetto family moves frequently, the moves are confined to their own turf. It's as if the devil has built a jail to confine them in their torment. Leaving is unthinkable. Fairy tale fantasies are the only escape from the concrete jungle, and they never come true.

I was only fifteen, but my dream of becoming "somebody" had already disappeared. But secretly, I still

41

wanted to become a doctor to heal my sick world. So, urged by an inner combination of destiny and adventure, I agreed to move to Philadelphia.

I placed only one demand on Alma: I had to meet Mom. I had dreamed about my mother hugging me for years, and now I wanted to see if it was possible. I wanted to confront the imagined with the real before I made the big move. My sisters had lived with her; I had seen her (though I did not know who she was), and Willie had followed her home. Now it was my turn. Curiosity demanded satisfaction.

Alma agreed quickly, she and Nettie had been trying to convince Mom to meet me for some time. She pleaded with Mom to see me, telling her of the mess my life had already become. Although she did not come right out and say it, Alma was suggesting that Mom's absence from my life had caused much of the problem. It was time for her to love her child. Mom finally agreed. She had divorced her new husband and the secret no longer needed to be kept. After Alma had loaded my things into her car for the move to Philadelphia, we went to meet her at a delicatessen across the street from where she worked.

Alma and I sat in a booth by the window and ordered a soda while we waited. Soon, the whistle at the factory blew and workers streamed into the streets. Finally, the lady who had given me candy appeared in the doorway and made her way to where we sat. She entered the humid little shop and walked to us. "Hello, little Luis."

I stood to my feet, even at fifteen I was nearly as tall as my short, little mother. "Hello, Mom," I replied, "How are you?"

For an awkward moment we faced each other. I did not know whether to hug her, shake her hand, or run. Mom had a forced grin in place and finally sat down beside me.

We ordered lunch and ate together. Glancing at her watch, she realized that it would soon be time to leave. In heavily-accented English, she spoke something of substance to me for the first time.

"Luis," she said, "I am sorry I haven't been part of your life. I hope you will understand someday. I do love you.

Alma tells me you're a troublemaker."

I was already uneasy, but when she said that, I slid a little lower under the table. I was a street-wise kid, but I had never been lectured by my real mother.

"Luis, I want you to be good as you go to live with Alma. Try your best to go to school and get good grades. Stay out of trouble, my son."

As we rose to leave, Mom put her arms around me and held me close. My arms hung loosely at my sides, and tears welled up in my eyes, but I was determined not to cry. Then she was gone. Alma and I watched her through the dirty window until she disappeared into the factory, then paid the check and got back into Alma's old car.

I felt empty as we drove across the George Washington Bridge into New Jersey. I had looked forward to today's meeting for years. Now the long-awaited event was history. I was glad to come face to face with my mother, but why did I feel so confused?

Realizing I was starting a brand new life, I turned and stared out the back window at the New York skyline. The lights were coming on in the skyscrapers and the city looked beautiful, but I knew better. I turned to see the big ball of fire setting in the west. Maybe, just maybe I'll be happy in Philadelphia. I flicked Alma's car radio on loudly and lit a cigarette.

Gail meets some of the Teen Challenge men who were in the program in Brazil

Chapter Six

The Shooting Gallery

Within 24 hours I was enrolled in school. Alma saw to that. Within 48 hours I found a new source for marijuana. I saw to that. Within 3 days I developed a steady relationship with a pretty, dark-eyed girl. She saw to that. Philadelphia and I became acquainted real fast.

I experienced several "firsts" in Philadelphia. The city of brotherly love is where I first experienced heroin, where I was introduced to big-time crime, where I first felt the course fiber of a prison uniform, and where I first tasted death. I gave my innocence to reality, my freedom to heroin addiction, my hopes to failure, and my family to despair.

Alma failed to tell me she was living with our uncle, Frank. Frank and his wife were kind people and very generous to allow me to live with them, but they had a number of children. But, the warm, homey atmosphere made me uneasy instead of welcomed. I was uncomfortable around Frank's happy family and, therefore, continued to spend most of my time on the street.

Frank gladly welcomed me into his home because of an

45

honest desire to help me outrun my problems. Frank was a Christian and had led Alma to accept Christ. They saw my move as an answer to prayer.

Frank's family was my first contact with real Christians. Their home was much different from what I was used to in the Bronx. Frank tolerated my lifestyle, even though we looked at life in completely different ways. In exchange for room and board, he only asked me to promise to attend church occasionally. Frank's happy family took some getting used to, but it was impossible for me to accept his church. Frank attended a Puerto Rican Pentecostal church full of emotion and enthusiasm.

I decided Frank's deal was fair and attended many services at first. The little band of believers met in a storefront hall, long ago abandoned by profitable business. Each arrival was greeted enthusiastically. Before being seated, each newcomer immediately found a place to kneel and pray at the crude altar splitting the gap between pulpit and pew. Earnestly and with great volume, they besought heaven for a few minutes before drying their tear-drenched eyes and settling in for the service. And I mean "settle in," because the sermons often lasted well over an hour. The people didn't mind, they simply laid their little-ones on a pallet under the pew and amened their approval as the preacher continued into the night.

Religion impressed me very little, but I admired the sincere devotion of these simple people and the way they loved their God. But I had no personal interest in their religion. I soon broke my agreement with Frank and stopped attending the loud little storefront church. Alma's commitment to Christ wavered, and she too stopped attending. I didn't feel too badly about not going back.

Though my increasingly deviant lifestyle had become evident to Frank, Alma refused to believe how serious my problems were becoming. She was completing her final semester of nurse's training and working full-time, so she was often unaware of my escapades. Alma refused to believe my troubles until the very end. She always believed little brother's alibis.

46

I spent most of my time on Fifth Street. The Philadelphia lifestyle was different from what I knew in the Bronx. There was very little gang activity, and we hung out in pool halls and bars instead of on street corners. My new world was made up of pushers, junkies, and car thieves.

This was more like it! I had never enjoyed the desperate violence of the Bronx, and I became very attracted to this new world. Anyone could see that lonely people lived behind the drugs, but the fantasy remained attractive to me.

My best friend was named Hector, and we spent most of our time shooting pool and hustling enough money to buy marijuana. One day our pusher, a guy named Julio, invited us to a party at a shooting gallery a few blocks away. Although we had heard about these palaces of drugs and sex, Hector and I had never visited one. Julio promised to show us a better way to get high. That sounded good to us, so we agreed to go.

I was shocked to discover that the glamorous shooting gallery was the dark, dirty basement of an abandoned tenement building. My fantasy had supposed that such a temple of sin would be a glittery, Las Vegas-type showcase where the gods of drugs and sex were openly worshipped. I was right about the open worship of drugs and sex, but I was completely wrong about the rest.

Hector and I stepped from the bright light of day down into the darkness. We stood blindly in the darkness until we were rudely greeted by the doorkeeper who demanded to know who we were. Suddenly our host, Julio, stepped up and said, "These are my friends. They're OK."

As our eyes adjusted to the darkness, we were able to survey the activities. A lone man was crouched before a water faucet that was sticking out of a crack in the wall, mixing up a fix. Another was slumped in a corner, just removing the needle from his arm, the belt still constricting the vein that had accepted the injection.

As we followed him down the hall, we passed a door that was open slightly. "Hector!" I whispered. Look at that couple gettin' it on."

"Wow! Isn't that something."

Couples were locked together in the dark room. While we watched, a couple rolled in their lust, she exposing her naked flesh before disappearing in the shadow of her lover.

I was quickly becoming nauseated by the smell of urine and body odor. The stench was overwhelming.

"Come over here, you guys," said Julio. "I have something to show you." Showing us to a room in the back of the filthy basement, he pulled three bags of white powder from his pocket.

Grinning broadly, he held the now white powder in his hand while his gold tooth glittered from the glare of the light bulb that dangled from a frayed cord. "This stuff is your ticket to paradise. You guys won't go back to grass after you've tried this stuff. This is the answer to all your problems."

Hector was gung-ho, but I was becoming uncomfortable. The "glamorous" shooting-gallery wasn't what I had expected. "Hey, man," I said, "that's great, but I'm a little short on cash."

"No problem!" he responded. He was in a generous mood. "You two are good customers, today's fix is on me. In fact, if you don't mind, I'll join you."

He laid the heroin on the table, took off his jacket, and began rolling up his shirt sleeves. He reached into his jacket pocket and took out the "works" we would need to shoot up.

"Hey, wait a minute," Hector said. "I don't want to get hooked on that stuff. I just want to get the buzz when I want to."

Hector and I had talked about doing heroin before, but we had seen too many spaced-out human hulls, lives ruined by heroin. We also knew the marks of an addict, the needle scars running up his arm like a disoriented railroad line. We weren't about to ruin our pretty bodies with needle marks. We were going to be "high class" recreational users. No drug was going to run our lives and turn us into dead-end junkies.

"OK, OK, leered Julio knowingly. "You don't have to inject the stuff to get the high. You can just snort it."

He, however, continued his preparations to shoot up. Carefully arranging his tools like a surgeon preparing for an operation, he lit a candle. After wiping the spoon on his dirty bluejeans, he poured it full of water from the wine bottle nearby. Now pouring the contents of one of the little bags into the spoon, he held the mixture over the flame until it boiled. Placing a small cotton ball in the solution, he removed the protective sheath from the needle and drew the concoction into the syringe. Uncoiling the rubber surgical hose, he tied it tightly around his upper arm, causing the veins to stand out like ropes.

Choosing a likely spot, he thrust the drug into his bloodstream. Almost immediately, euphoria swept over his countenance as he slipped into another world. We watched silently for a few moments as he became accustomed to his new surroundings.

"Its your turn," he said, weakly lifting his eyelids. Unfolding the matchbook cover, he carefully poured a row of the white powder along its crease. I took it from his hand and held it under my nostril. It looked like powdered sugar and burned as I sucked it into my body. Slowly, happiness worked its way to my extremities. I felt the most immense high I had ever known. Smiling from the glow, I watched Hector take his snort and join me.

Julio made his way back into the main room while Hector and I basked in the rush. Finally, levelling from the peak of the drug's acceleration and riding the sustained high, we made our way out of the shooting gallery.

"Come back soon!" Julio called after us.

"We will, we will," we chorused as we stepped back into the real world. We weren't being polite; we had found a better escape route, and we planned to use it often. The dirty streets of the noisy city didn't seem to matter anymore. I was on a flight to another world, a better world.

We snorted heroin for a few weekends, leaving marijuana behind for the better high. I was buying a couple of bags weeks later when Julio asked me how I was enjoying my new "friend." I told him I was enjoying it very much, but that I was finding my new pleasure very expensive.

"You're wasting it, man," he responded. "You need to shoot it up and quit leaving so much up your nose."

"No way," I shot back. I wasn't about to mark my body up and become some pusher's profit machine.

"Hey, you don't have to mainline, just try a little skin-popping," he said. "Come on down to the store and I'll show you how."

A few weeks before I wouldn't have considered putting a needle in my skin, but I was enjoying the new high so much I agreed. After all, it wasn't like I was mainlining. I was just going to get a better high for my dollar.

Skin-popping is piercing the skin just deeply enough to inject the drug. While not as direct as driving the drug straight into the vein, skin-popping produces a quicker and better high than snorting. I met Julio at the shooting gallery the next day and he showed me the ropes. He even supplied me with a free set of "works." After all, I was a good investment.

I was really beginning to enjoy my new lifestyle and the fantasies heroin provided, but detested the kind of person I had become. I completely disregarded Willie's best advice. Willie had been a really bad dude, but he had never done drugs and always looked down on those who chained their life to chemicals. Here was Willie's little brother, strung out and loving every minute of it.

All my friends were junkies. Every weekend was spent "goofing" together. Goofing is the riotous and disoriented "fun" of a bunch of people who are high on drugs. People goofing can get really strange. Everyone's drugs become community property and are thrown into a witch's brew with deathly potential. Everyone reacts differently to the devil's candy. Several will simply sit around in circles, talking, laughing, and telling increasingly outrageous jokes. As the night continues, everthing becomes funny, and the circle becomes a wildly confused group of fools. Some simply stare into space, tuned to some demonically transmitted signal. Others plunge wildly into illicit sexual encounters.

We did most of our weekend goofing in a city park at 4th and Huntington Streets. Weekend nights found us in groups scattered throughout the park, obviously high. Alma was dating a policeman who had been trying to convince her how mixed up I had become. Alma wanted to believe only the best about her flesh and blood and refused to believe him. In deference to Alma, he left me alone, but he had seen me high several times.

On a warm evening of my fifteenth summer, Alma and her policeman-boyfriend drove to the park to witness the depths of my depravity first-hand. Suddenly, as they watched from across the street, a police van screeched to the curb, lights flashing. In a moment, our mid-summer's night's revelry turned to a nightmare.

Like rats fleeing a burning warehouse, we sprayed in every direction, tossing drugs into the shrubbery as we darted away. Very few escaped, however, and soon I lay belly-down on the lush green grass.

For the first time, I felt the cold steel of chrome handcuffs squeeze rings around my wrists. The policemen huddled triumphantly over their prisoners, awaiting the arrival of reinforcements. The intensity of a heroin induced high is rivalled only by the destitution of being busted. I was rapidly plunging toward the bottom, unable and unwilling to stop myself.

Chapter Seven

Down, Down, Down

I found myself in jail for the first time. I called my sister Alma and tried to convince her that I had been framed. I was conning and jiving her around, trying to convince her that I had just been in the wrong place at the wrong time.

"You need to come get me," I said. "It's only a $500 bail, you would just have to come up with $50 to spring me. Come get me, I can't take this. I've heard a lot of bad things about being here in the detention center."

She said that she would have to think about it, so I sat down in the processing hall. It takes them hours and I had to sit by a lot of mean dudes. The guy beside me had just committed armed robbery. I was not that bad yet, I was just a beginner in for my first arrest.

I heard them talking, and I said that I was not going to allow myself to get that bad. They were saying that they had messed up by not going ahead and killing the guy so he couldn't finger them.

I was really scared. Finally, they called my name to go to the orientation block where you stay three to five days before being assigned to your permanent cell block. They led us down the catwalk to the cell that had been assigned to me.

As I walked by the other cells, the inmates shouted at me. "Hey, man, wha' cha in for?" Others shouted, "There goes a new one!"

When I reached the door of my cell, the guard in the control booth flipped the switch that opened the bars. I stepped inside and they automatically clanged shut behind me. Suddenly I felt trapped like a caged animal.

I crashed on my bunk until they sounded the horn for supper. Suddenly, all the cells automatically opened. As I stood in the line for supper, I began to see the look of lust in eyes that were glaring at me.

I began to hear them whisper to one another, "If he's in here long, we'll take his manhood or make him buy his protection." My friends who had spent time in jail warned me how the inmates raped newcomers.

When I finally got to the mess hall and sat down, some other Puerto Rican guys came and sat beside me. "Hey, Luis," they said, "don't worry about it. We know what you are going through. We're here and we're going to take care of you. The word is already going out that no one is to mess with you or they will answer to us. You're gonna be O.K."

"Hey, man," I responded, "I appreciate all the help I can get."

"Yea, those guys aren't gonna mess with you. You're one of us, and we stick together." I hoped they meant what they said, because those guys were still looking me over.

I didn't stay in jail long. I swore I would never do drugs again, that I would straighten out my life, that I would once again control the dreams of my mind and the cravings of my body. But, my resolutions would fail. I was no longer in control.

I possessed no drugs at the time of arrest, so I was booked on a misdemeanor charge of public intoxication. I was a first time offender, so sentencing was suspended. The rest of my friends were released within a few days and the next weekend found us in another spot, goofing again.

The arrest changed me. I no longer feared the police. I

resumed using drugs with more intensity and less fear of punishment. I also gained a greater respect from my buddies. Being in trouble with the police is a badge of honor.

Hector soon talked me into mainlining. I was hooked, and I knew it. If I was going to have to ride this train of death, I decided to go first class.

Mainlining heroin had advantages and disadvantages over snorting and skin-popping. I achieved a much greater high per dollar than before, and the rush was fantastic. No one ever takes so much heroin that he doesn't get a rush as the powder speeds through his veins. The disadvantage became clear after the first few days: this was going to be expensive. In the beginning I spent about $20 per day on drugs. Soon after beginning to mainline heroin, my bill became $100 every day.

Once again, I convinced Alma that I really wanted to go straight. She pulled a few strings at the hospital and I was hired as an orderly. The University Medical Center is a huge complex containing thousands of beds. I ran errands for the doctors and kept the supplies in order.

Alma wasn't the only one who was fooled. I knew I was in trouble, but I still thought I was destined to become somebody. I was a high school dropout with a record, but I was still convinced I was someone special.

Working at University Medical Center fulfilled my dream to be a doctor. I wasn't a doctor, but I was helping heal people. I worked very hard at my job and soon became a trusted member of the staff. The doctors and nurses knew I would give them the reliable assistance they needed to save lives. I was even trusted to perform some basic medical services such as preparing patients for surgery and closing an incision. I wasn't qualified for these jobs, but I had shown my dependability and had learned how.

Many of the doctors were as messed up as I was. Working long hours under tremendous stress, some of them had taken advantage of their easy access to drugs. Their drugs had more sophisticated names and more legitimate uses, but they had the same problem I did.

I had access to the drug supplies and occassionally tried various pills. I had reached the point that I would take virtually anything to get high. Other times I sold the stolen drugs to buy heroin.

I had achieved a reputation for dependable and capable service and was on call for the entire hospital. Most of the orderlies were assigned to specific floors or tasks, but I wore a pager and was summoned anytime someone needed my services. This was great until I began to work many, many hours of overtime. Working 50 to 60 hours a week put me under a lot of stress and I found it difficult to stay awake. When I complained to some of the doctors they suggested I do what they did when they had to pull a long shift; just find an empty room and take a nap.

This should have been the greatest time of my life. I was respected in my profession, I was making lots of money, and my future looked bright. In reality, however, I had absolutely no respect for myself. Every dime I was making and what I could steal was winding up in the pocket of my pusher, and I was always broke. I should have cried out for help, but my pride and what pleasure I was getting from the drugs wouldn't let me.

I finally began shooting heroin at work. Wearing long-sleeved shirts so no one could see the needle marks on my arms, I did my best to cover up. Any spare moment found me hiding in an out of the way place, trying to catch a few moments sleep or sticking a needle in my arm. When I was high, the beep of the pager just annoyed me and I began turning it off. I hid in vacant rooms for hours, oblivious to the fact that most of the hospital was looking for me. When I came out, I insisted that I had been on another floor with another doctor. They always believed my alibis because the hospital was so huge.

As the final weeks of my employment spun by, it became apparent to all that something was dreadfully wrong with Luis Torres. I had moved completely away from Alma and seldom saw her. I staggered into work late every day and was of little help. I had previously been able to perform intricate medical procedures, but now I had difficulty running errands. I was finally caught when a doctor who had unsuccessfully attempted to locate me staggered dead-tired into the room where I was shooting heroin. With one glance he understood everything. My disheveled condition, the pager in the off position, and my wild eyes made it apparent that what they feared was true. I was fired immediately.

The job was all that held my life together, and I went from worse to worst. I blamed the entire affair on my superiors at work, saying they had fired me without justification. A drug addict won't admit that he alone is responsible for his actions. Drugs are his master; he is completely out of control.

My days became spent wandering the streets, killing time between fixes. Life became just a series of needle pricks. It's no wonder that I soon overdosed. When you are in love with the devil you don't know when to stop.

I still kept in loose contact with some of my friends in New York who were big drug dealers. A junkie makes a terrible pusher, so I never took advantage of my old contacts. But one day, when I was buying a fix from my pusher, Pedro Juan, I heard him complain that he needed a new source. I told him I could lead him to some good stuff in exchange for drugs. He was delighted with the arrangement and we and my friend Tarzan made a trip to New York City to buy a new supply.

Pedro Juan, Tarzan, and I returned from New York City with $5,000 worth of pure, uncut, heroin. Tarzan was one of my closest friends. We called him that because he was well built. We walked up the stairs to Pedros Juan's apartment over the grocery store. I had to wait in the hall. Pedro Juan's family did not know his true profession and he never let them see the junkies he did business with.

After a few moments, he returned with my cut. He told us to split. I was tired and sick, and long overdue for my fix.

"You guys hurry up, shoot up and get out of here. Don't you know it's five in the morning? My family will be up soon and I don't want my old lady and kids to see you here."

He angrily thrust some works into my hand and slammed the door. We sat down on the stairway landing and got ready to shoot up. I filled a bottle cap with some of the water from the glass Pedro Juan had given us and added the heroin. I was so sleepy that I forgot this was pure stuff, no powdered milk had been added to cut its purity.

I placed two pinches of heroin into the water and held the cap with a hair pin while Tarzan heated the solution with a match. When the solution had boiled and the powder had dissolved completely, I pulled the solution through the needle into the syringe. Tarzan took his belt off and wrapped it tightly around my upper arm, making the veins of my forearm bulge in anticipation.

I was weak and shaking as the needle approached its mark. Tarzan was telling me to hurry up because he wanted to get off. I usually felt a rush when the drug went into my veins, but the next thing I knew, Tarzan was slapping my face screaming, "Wake up man, wake up!" I felt like I was on a slow motion merry-go-round as the world was spun around me.

Suddenly, the door flew open. There stood Pedro Juan, cursing. "What's going on out here!"

Tarzan shouted, "He's OD'ing, man! He's gonna die! Get some salt water!"

He ran back in the apartment to get the salt water. They immediately injected it into my veins, hoping it would help.

I was really in a buzz, slowly realizing that I was in trouble. I vaguely sensed that I was wet from the water they had thrown on me to wake me up. Having been a drug addict for two and one-half years, I was aware that I had overdosed.

Pedro Juan had no compassion. He just wanted me out of there; and now! Tarzan was so strong that he grabbed me and slung me over his shoulder, taking me down to the street. He swung the doorway open and we stepped into the first light of dawn.

"Let's go, Luis. We've got to keep you awake, or you'll die, man." I walked like a drunk man as he held me in his arms.

"What happened?" I asked.

"You took too much, man, and I'm sick and need to shoot up. C'mon, wake up so I can get fixed."

We walked a half mile to Indiana Street. I was still dizzy, but I realized what had happened. Tarzan was getting mad because he had to walk all that way craving his own fix. We stopped at some friends' house and knocked until they came to the door.

"Hey, man, Luis has just taken an overdose," he said, "and I've got to get fixed. Stay with him so I can take care of myself."

"Don't you even think of dying on us," my friends said as Tarzan disappeared into the house. Finally, around ten o'clock that morning, I was past the point of danger and went into the house and crashed.

If Tarzan hadn't been a friend, Pedro Juan would have been stuck with a corpse on his doorstep; and that's bad for a pusher's business. I should have sworn off drugs after a bad scene like that, but when I woke up, my first thought was, "That was really strong stuff. I need to get some more of that, but I need to be more careful how much I shoot."

That was the best stuff I had ever used, I had just taken too much. I staggered to my feet and stumbled off to find Pedro Juan to get another fix.

Many came for a touch from God in the Brazil Crusade

Chapter Eight

Life Of Crime

Coming up with a hundred dollars every day is difficult for anyone, especially for a sixteen year old Puerto Rican. The overdose scared me, but not badly enough to make me kick the habit. Before long, I was worse than ever. I must have quit a thousand times, but never for over 24 hours.

Since no job I qualified for would pay one hundred dollars a day, I faced a choice, either kick the habit or turn to crime. Kicking the habit was even more impossible than making an honest one hundred dollars a day, so I turned to crime.

I had tried petty street crimes such as purse snatching and stick-ups but realized they were too dangerous. Besides, old ladies didn't carry the kind of money I needed. So the next logical step was burglary.

I became a very accomplished burglar, but when I began, I was very gullible. I was keeping company with a rough gang of guys who were older than I. Being the youngest, I felt privileged to be in their presence. I didn't realize they were using me. Around noon we went through the telephone directory, looking for a home in a neighborhood that would likely yield a lot of loot. When they found a likely house where no one answered the telephone, they would park down the street and wait while I went in and did the job. It didn't take me long to realize that I could do the job just as well alone and keep all of the money instead of splitting with my older friends.

From that time on, I committed most burglaries either alone or with one friend. Still a loner, I didn't like to work too closely with other junkies. It was hard to come up with the kind of money I needed alone, much less when I had to split the take with accomplices. We marketed the stolen goods through a fence or pawn shop. Many pawn shops asked no questions unless you brought in an extremely rare or valuable piece. The fence would buy anything. We were lucky to get ten cents on the dollar of the retail value of an item though. This meant that I had to steal at least $1,000 worth of goods every day just to stay even.

I worked the day shift most often during my career as a burglar. Daytime afforded the most anonymity because the occupants were at work. Before long I had a system worked out. I would call a likely house for several days to determine a pattern of the times the occupants were gone. Then, I would enter the neighborhood early in the morning and find a place to hide until everyone in the house had left for school or work. Then I entered through a door or window and ransacked the place.

I could work my way through a house very quickly after I had learned the most frequently used hiding places. I looked for electronic equipment, silver, and cash first. I got so good at burlarizing homes I could steal a radio and leave the music behind!

A burglar has absolutely no respect for the private property of others. Quickly making my way through the house, I tore open cabinet and closet doors, raking my arms across the shelves and dashing the items to the floor, stopping only to pick up the valuable pieces. Ransacking the bedroom, I snatched the clothes out of the closets, jerked drawers out of the furniture, and hurled mattresses from the beds. Many whose homes have been burglarized say they feel as if they have been raped. The two acts of crime are similar, the junkie pilfering a home has no respect for anyone but the vulture on his veins. He violates anything to satisfy the craving.

Occasionally, when I was desperate or when an especially good home was always occupied during the day, I entered a home at night. I burglarized several homes while the family was asleep, oblivious that a desperate addict was stealing their prized possessions. I did very little of this, however. I still had a strong aversion to violence, especially when I would be the recipient if the homeowner awoke and found me present!

One of the scariest episodes occurred during a midnight raid. Upon entering, I realized the family was home, so I was being very careful. I made my way through the kitchen and the dining room, slipping the box of silver under my arm. As I turned to go up the stairs, I saw someone in the shadows. It was too dark to see who it was, but I had no trouble recognizing the shotgun he pointed at my head.

"What do you think you're doing, punk?" he asked.

I was too afraid to respond. I stood frozen in fright, realizing that at any moment I could become a memory. I also knew that the man would be in no trouble with the law; in fact, the Philadelphia police would probably thank him for ridding the streets of one more hoodlum.

Seeing I wasn't going to answer, the man took a step or two toward me, gun ready. I had no idea what to do, so I stood paralyzed with fear. Amazingly, in those few milliseconds, the thought crossed my mind, "What will Mom and Papi think when they get the news that their son was killed in a burglary!"

When he was within six or eight feet, the man spoke again. "You Puerto Rican trash! Put my stuff down and get out of my house, or I'll blow your brains out!"

I couldn't see the man's eyes in the darkness, but I knew he meant business. One glance down the barrel of the shotgun convinced me he was serious. Dropping the silver with a clatter I scampered out of the house and out the door. I ran as fast as I could for several blocks, finally stopping and leaning against a corner street lamp. Although it was a hot July night, I shook like a leaf. After several attempts to strike a match, I finally lit a joint and took a deep drag. It took several minutes to collect myself.

I later heard that the man's home had been burglarized previously. He had received virtually no help from the police. In fact, it was the next day before they even came to investigate. He decided that the police were helpless. He was right, the Philadelphia police department will receive dozens of burglary reports on any given night, only a small percentage of which are ever solved. Why the man didn't pull the trigger I will never know.

A daylight burglary set up by a tip from friends was the most lucrative I ever took part in. One night, several of us were hanging around a pool hall in north Philly. We were strung out on heroin and were talking about how we could raise some cash. A couple of other guys were hanging out with us who were just casual drug users and had daytime jobs. We began talking about some of the crimes we had been pulling when one of them told of a house that we should hit. His old lady was friends with some elderly people who had been saving up for retirement. They had $5,000 hidden in the house. The old folks had even gone so far as to tell where they hid the money; under the mattress, in denominations of fives, tens, and twenties.

Needless to say, we decided to hit this house as soon as possible. Since there were four of us who heard the tip at the same time, we decided that it was only fair that we all shared in the money and in responsiblility for the job. After casing the house for two days, we found out that both husband and wife worked and that they left for work at the same time every morning and returned home at the same time every evening. The next day would be the day.

At around eleven o'clock we began approaching the house, each from a different direction at a different time. It wasn't any trouble to get in, the door was unlocked! I was the last to enter, and when I came into the kitchen, I found my friends devouring a huge feast. It was common for us to raid the refrigerator if we were hungry during a job, often leaving dirty dishes and food on the table, but these guys were really pigging out. All of us were high, so we acted like we owned the place, eating everything in sight, oblivious to the possibility of getting caught.

When we had our fill, we began working our way through the house, picking up trinkets and stuffing them into our pockets. When we got to the bedroom we overturned the mattress, and there, just as we had been told, lay the money in small bills. It looked like we had walked into the vault at First National Bank. Hector grabbed two handfulls and flung the bills into the air, laughing like a child. Everyone followed suit and soon the air was filled with green paper. Finally, coming to our senses, we began stuffing the bills into our shirts and trousers.

We left the house en masse, foolishly brazen, and walked away so as not to arouse suspicion. As we were walking down the alley behind the row of houses, the neighbor who was raking his little patch of lawn saw us.

"Hey, you kids," he shouted. "What are you doing in that house?"

"We were just visiting my uncle," I returned.

"What are they doing home today," he responded, "why aren't they at work?"

"Spanish Independence Day, old man," I shouted. "Don't you know everybody gets off for Spanish Independence Day?"

"Oh yea, I guess you're right," he mumbled and turned back to his raking.

When we got out of sight we began to run, not stopping until we reached the park. Rolling in the grass, laughing until our sides hurt, we celebrated our success.

"Spanish Independence Day! Man, Torres, you're too much," they hooted.

When we could finally talk, we wiped the tears of laughter from our eyes and put all of the money in a pile, dividing it in four equal shares.

My share lasted a week.

Chapter Nine

Mom Knows

"This is a pretty nice car don't you think, Willie?"

"Yea, this is a great car, Luis. That must be a pretty good job you have to be able to afford a car like this. And you trade so often, too."

Willie and I were speeding down the New Jersey Turnpike one August afternoon in a stolen Dodge Charger that was just like new. All junkies are good at covering their habit, but I was better than most. I had my family convinced that I had a good job with a business man and that some of the cars I drove were his and some of them were mine. During the past few months I had begun stealing more automobiles instead of burglarizing homes.

I found car thievery more profitable and easier than ransacking a home and working with a wide array of pawn shops and fences. Stealing a car was very easy compared with the hassle of breaking and entering a house, and I just had to deal with one man to turn the car into cash.

About two or three nights a week I had some of my buddies drop me off in a likely neighborhood. I wandered around, looking for a luxury car or for a model like my fence was looking for. Very few people even locked their cars, so I always found what I wanted. I would have it running within seconds and drive away. I took the cars to the fence the next morning if I needed the money immediately, but if I had any reserve, I drove them around for a few days, particularly if it was a beautiful model. The police never looked for a particular model and color, they only looked for the license number of a stolen car. That presented no problem; I just replaced the car's license plate with one I had stolen off of another car.

I was stopped several times for various minor traffic violations while driving stolen cars. You can imagine why when you consider that I was just 16 or 17 years old at the time and didn't even have a driver's license. Besides that, I was usually on some drug that altered my reflexes. I was never seriously questioned, however. This was before the days when the police used the computer extensively and I would always give them some excuse why I didn't have my driver's license with me. I don't think the police wanted to go to the trouble of making an arrest anyway, so I was never caught.

It amazes the law-abiding citizen that this underworld system of car thievery really works. Young punks like me steal these cars to support their habit. At that time new cars were selling for between $4,000 and $10,000. After stealing a car, I would take it to a chop shop. After pulling the car inside, the man would walk around it appraising its value. Some of the models were more valuable to repaint and replace their serial number plate with one from a wrecked car in order to sell them again. Thousands of Americans never suspect that they are driving "hot" cars, but they are. Other models are more valuable when sold in pieces for replacement parts and they are dismantled, thus the term, "chop shop." I sold most of the cars I stole for between $300 and $700. That's not much money for a $7,000 car, but when you only have one outlet, you take what he will give. Besides, that kept me going for as much as a week. That sure beat burglarizing a home every day just to stay alive. I stole over 250 cars before finally landing in jail for the last time.

On this particular afternoon, Willie and I had decided to go into Jersey to have some fun. Willie was now a corporal in the army and was spending some time at home on leave. We were cruising down the turnpike drinking beer, the twin exhaust pipes rumbling their throaty roar in our wake. Suddenly, we heard the ominous "thump, thump, thump" of a flat tire. As I pulled to the side of the highway, Willie said, "Well, give me the key to the trunk and I'll put the spare on. It shouldn't take long."

Little did Willie know that I didn't have a trunk key. I had stolen the car a few days ago by using a master key and had absolutely no way to get into the trunk.

"I'm sorry, Willie," I said, "I don't have a trunk key."

"What do you mean! You don't have a trunk key to your own car!"

"Yea, well, I loaned the car to my girlfriend last week and she lost the trunk key."

Willie believed my story. We got out of the car and stood on the shoulder for a while, unsure of what to do. I was beginning to become a little afraid, after all, how was I going to get into the trunk and what if someone stopped to help and discovered that the car was stolen? Finally, I decided we would have to flag a passing motorist, even if it was a risk.

It wasn't long before a car pulled in behind to help us. But this car wasn't just an ordinary car. It was black and white and had a flashing red light on top. Just my luck! After breaking down in a stolen car, I was going to be assisted by a New Jersey State Trooper!

Luckily, Willie was dressed in his army uniform, so the trooper was more kind to us than he otherwise might have been.

"What's the problem here, guys?" he asked. "Is there some way I can be of help?"

Willie walked up to him like a real gentleman. "Yea, officer, you can help us. We have a flat on the car, and my dumb brother over there has lost the trunk key to his own car."

69

I have never been so frightened in all my life! Here we were, stuck on the New Jersey Turnpike, Willie and I both had a record and a flat tire on a stolen car!

As crazy as it sounds, the trooper took a liking to us and spent the rest of the afternoon helping us. Taking a tire tool out of his own trunk he removed our flat, loaded it into his patrol car and took us several miles to the nearest service station. We left the tire with the attendant who promised to get to it as soon as possible. The trooper invited us to go next door and have a bite to eat with him while we waited. Willie and the cop had a great conversation, but he probably thought I was the shy and silent type; I was too scared to say a word!

After finishing our meal, we returned next door to discover that the tire was damaged beyond repair. We had no cash and the station owner was reluctant to take Willie's check as payment for a new tire. The trooper helped us persuade the man to take Willie's check and soon we were on our way back to the car, a newly mounted tire in the trunk of the patrol car. When we reached the car, the trooper remounted the tire and bade us farewell. Only years later did I tell Willie the car was stolen.

I had many, many girlfriends during this period. I was never at a loss for female companionship when I wanted it. But, when a drug addict is at his worst he is oblivious of almost all basic needs, including food, sleep, and female companionship. I had begun keeping close company with a girl named Mary. My mother and sisters hated Mary from the beginning.

Mary was a tall, lithe blonde with a lily-white complexion. My family wanted to see me only with dark-eyed Puerto Rican girls. Besides this, they had the impression that Mary was the root of my deepening troubles. In reality, I was a bad influence on Mary. But even during my worst troubles, the family wanted to believe that I was a victim of circumstances and the bad advice of bad company.

My mother was in the city and spent a lot of the time with my sister Nettie.

The Puerto Rican neighborhoods are 24 hour a day communities. Any hour finds activities in the street involving the youngest to the oldest. Children play and the teens gather on the street corners to listen to music, talk, and laugh. The middle-aged will often drag the dining room tables into the narrow streets, setting up liquor and beer to have a party. The musicians play lively, loud Latin music while couples whirl to the beat. The aged sit on the stoop, nodding their heads to the familiar songs.

One day Mary walked past Mom's house. Mom and Nettie had perched on the stoop to watch the children play and were discussing my problem. When Mom saw Mary she began to scream, "There she is! There's the cheap whore who is leading my son to an early grave!"

Mary had heard it all before and couldn't take it any more. She grabbed my mother and started yelling. Screaming and crying, Nettie pried them apart.

"I'm not the devilish influence that is destroying your son! I wasn't the one who made a junkie out of him. Luis was strung out with needle tracks down his arm long before I met him, and your son is gonna die a junkie. You're just too stupid to believe the truth!"

"Shut up!" Mom shouted. "You are the one who has corrupted my son! You will be the death of him!"

By this time, a small crowd had gathered, gawking eyes were taking in every verbal blow. Backed into a corner, Mary instinctively struck back with all of the defense she could muster.

"Do you want proof? I'll show you proof. Come with me," Mary commanded.

Mom was mad enough to agree and, pulling Nettie by the arm, she followed Mary down the street. The gaping neighbors parted like the water as they strode down the sidewalk.

Down the block to the corner they hurried after the winsome blonde, then to the left and down that block, crossing against the light in their rush. Sensing the ominous tone of the ever increasing procession as it passed, those leaning against the buildings hushed their talk as the parade hurried by. Only the sounds of the various machines in the buildings warbled on as they passed. A window fan droned, the bass-note thump of a juke box rhythmically continued, and the crying of a baby mingled with the sounds of the traffic. Silently, the onlookers gawked at the skinny blond with the fine hair flying in the breeze followed by the stout, middle-aged, Puerto Rican woman and her entourage.

Stopping on the corner, Mary turned her face skyward and shouted, "Luis Torres! Come down from there. I know you are in there, come down right now!"

I didn't hear their calls. I was sitting on a stairway landing outside Pedro Juan's apartment and had just pulled a needle from my arm. I was sitting in the exact same spot where I had overdosed.

Pedro Juan heard Mary loud and clear though. He was the proprietor of this, the largest shooting gallery in North Philly. This was publicity he didn't need.

The nondescript two story building on the corner looked like a quaint little Mom and Pop grocery. The lower story was devoted to vegetables, milk, and bread, but the second story was the headquarters of the biggest pusher in town.

By now a good sized crowd had gathered. Everyone in the neighborhood knew the real business transacted at this address, and silently they congregated to see what was going on. Suddenly, an upstairs window flew open, and Pedro Juan stuck his head out, angrily demanding an explanation for all the racket. Seeing Pedro Juan, Mary immediately ran down the street, calling over her shoulder, "Just ask him, lady. He'll tell you all about your sweet little boy!"

Quickly sizing up the situation, Mom was furious. Her smoldering anger burst into flame. The absurd shouting match was on. My short, plump, little Mom was planted in the middle of the intersection, snarling traffic in four directions, hands on broad hips, screaming for satisfaction. Pedro Juan, knowing that the increasingly rowdy crowd would soon attract the police, suddenly slammed the window and hurried down the steps, pulling a handgun from his belt.

Pointing the weapon as he stepped from the doorway of the building, he pointed it at Mom and began to scream obscenities, commanding her to leave the corner, declaring that her son was not there.

When she refused to budge, Pedro Juan decided he would rather lose a customer than his business and ducked into the darkness, returning with me in tow. Delivering me to my mother, he instructed everyone to leave, and with one wave of the pistol, it was done.

Weeping, Mom dragged me home. "Why, my son, why!" she sobbed. Wailing as if a loved one had died, she and Nettie wet my hair with their tears. I was so high that I didn't understand what was going on. I struggled to my feet, tears in my own eyes and shook free. While they pulled at my clothes, I pushed toward the door of the narrow house, stumbling through Nettie's collection of wide-eyed babies.

I finally reached the stoop and turned to look back inside. Tears streaming down their faces, Mom and Nettie looked deep into my eyes, very confused. They were not nearly so confused as I. Stepping into the street I slammed the door behind me.

Chapter Ten

Maria

I spent the next six months on the streets. Everyday was a new address, every meal a new discovery. I really didn't need a place to live, just a place to crash. I really didn't need much food either. A junkie becomes kind of like a wino when it comes to food, he loses all appetite. But, at least the wino gets the nutrients of the bottle, the junkie just wastes away.

Days were spent nodding away on some street corner or in the dark confines of a neighborhood bar with my best friend at the time, a Puerto Rican guy named Lefty. At night I roamed the sidestreets, looking for a car to steal. My life became like an animal's, stalking all night, sleeping all day. The only reason I lived was to survive. Death seemed a viable alternative.

I had been doing heroin for four long years now, and the drug had taken its toll on my mind and body. Occasionally I would vow to change. Even girls lost their appeal to me until I met a young lady named Maria. I was on one of my short, periodic improvement periods when I met her. Maybe she saw the possibilities in my life that were briefly shining through while I was trying to become something besides a walking corpse. During those times when I tried to straighten out, I would reduce, but never eliminate, my heroin use. There was no way to eliminate the stranglehold the drug had on my body.

Maria's father was considered a wealthy man among the Puerto Rican people of North Philly. He owned several neighborhood grocery stores and a growing wholesale produce business. I often stopped by their store to see Maria and would pitch in and help unload trucks. True to form, I was charming and endearing when I wasn't too strung out. My basic personality was still there under all the layers of hate.

It seemed like I was on the devil's torture rack. I wanted to do good, to kick the habit and go straight, but couldn't do anything but what I was doing. I was pulled from one side by the desire to be something besides the disaster I was, and from the other by the evil that constantly sang its siren song to my spirit. Daylight found me resolving to do better, night found me on the prowl to steal one more Cadillac.

My car thieving ways finally caught up with me one winter night. I had stolen a yellow GTO the night before and was cruising the streets. In a heroin haze, I ran a traffic light and was pulled to the side by two members of Philadelphia's finest. By chance one of them recalled seeing an all-points-bulletin on just such a car and radioed headquarters for verification. Sure enough, it was the car I was driving and I was arrested.

This was my first arrest in some time, and I thought lightly of it, knowing I would soon be back on the streets like before. My friends and I had absolutely no respect for the police. We had skipped bail and been released under assumed names so many times that we had lost all fear of the courts. One time, one of my buddies was arrested for driving a stolen car and was taken to the station house in the squad car while the other officer drove the stolen car and parked it in front of the headquarters building as evidence. While the two policemen booked my friend, we restole the stolen car. Not only did the police have to release our buddy for lack of evidence, they lost the car because we went straight to the chop shop and sold it.

I did have to await arraignment though and was placed in a holding cell. I had been ill for several days, and during the time I was in jail I became deathly sick. I was taken to the doctor where it was determined that I had hepatitis from using a dirty injection needle. By this time I was hallucinating and had no idea where I was. I was immediately transferred to Philadelphia General Hospital, my former employer.

I had a strong and immediate reaction to hepatitis because I had been afflicted with it before. Hepatitis is the disease of the junkie. A case of jaundice sometimes comes with it. Within a few days the worst was over and I became aware of where I was. Hepatitus is known as "yellow fever" because of the affect it has on the skin pigment. My case was an unusually severe case and my skin turned a very vivid yellow. The hospital was using very pale yellow sheets and some dumb orderly put a yellow hospital gown on me. With all that yellow, I looked like a Chiquita banana!

Regardless of my sickness, I was still in a lot of trouble with the law, and they were afraid of escape. They needn't have feared, I was so weak I couldn't have pushed the elevator button. The police department did, however, station a guard at the end of the hall 24 hours a day. Even though they knew I was too weak to flee, they realized some of my buddies might try to get me out. Apparently, I was in big trouble this time.

My buddies didn't try to kidnap me, but they did sneak drugs to me. The doctors couldn't figure out why I wasn't going through withdrawal. Some of my junkie friends were climbing the fire escape and slipping me heroin and the works to shoot up with.

Maria and her father came to see me as soon as I was able to have visitors. Maria really loved me. She was a beautiful young girl, with deep-brown, almond-shaped eyes and a pleasant smile. I had been lying to her ever since we had been seeing one another. When she came to see me in the hospital, I told her that I was innocent, that I had just borrowed the car from a friend, not knowing that it was stolen. She believed me, and with big tears falling from her high cheekbones she told me she loved me.

Her father was a very proper man, dressed in a conservative suit. He stood holding his hat in his hand as he watched his daughter take my hand. I could read the skepticism in his eyes as he stepped to the side of my bed, but his love for his daughter was even more evident as he began to speak.

"Luis," he began, "my daughter loves you very much. My daughter means everything in the world to me and her happiness is my one desire. I have seen you around my business, you have a good way with people. Luis, do you love my daughter?"

I cared for Maria, but was it love? I doubted it really, but, caught up in the emotion of the moment, I told him that I did. My nature left me totally incapable of destroying this lovely creature that obviously cared very much for me.

Leaning closer, he continued. "If you love her, I will offer you a management position with my company. We'll see how it works out; maybe you two will even get married."

"Daddy," Maria spoke through her happy glow, "can't we get Luis out of this situation he's in. He's really innocent."

"Yes, I'll see what I can do about arranging Luis's bail," he responded. No price was too high to pay for the happiness of his treasure.

As he backed toward the door, Maria leaned to kiss me. As her lips brushed against my cheek a hot tear fell from the pool in her eyes and saltily landed on my lips.

By the next morning I was feeling well enough to be returned to the jail. When I arrived, I was taken to the front desk. Shaking his head in disbelief, the desk sergeant said I was free on bail. Grinning as I took the pen from his hand, I signed the papers that would again make me a free man. When I returned his pen, he raised his eyebrows and pointed toward the street.

I should have been ecstatic. I was free! But, was I? Hardly. I was imprisoned by the lies a pretty Puerto Rican girl believed. The bounty that made me a fugitive was the bail paid by her adoring daddy.

Conflicting thoughts raced through my mind as I stood on the steps of the jailhouse. Should I go to Maria or should I continue to live on the run? I had no choice. If I went to Maria and her father, I would have to face trial for the charges filed against me. There was no way I could beat the rap. I was clearly guilty. I only had one choice. I ran.

The fact that I lied to a gullible young lady who loved me shows the depth of my depravity. I know I hurt her deeply, but I would only have hurt her more had I stayed and the courts found me guilty.

I was safe until my court date arrived. After I failed to show, I once again became a fugitive. That kind of life was nothing new though. I had lived like a fugitive for a long time. Constantly looking over your shoulder isn't any way to live, but it beats being in jail.

I returned to car theft and petty crime to support myself. By this time I had dwindled to 140 pounds and was very sick. I had no desire for food or anything else; I only desired the drugs that were destroying me.

Not only did I still have my $100 a day habit to support, I had run up several thousand dollars in debt from the drugs I consumed while in the hospital. My pusher was glad to see to it that I got the drugs I craved even though I didn't have any money. A pusher knows a good investment when he sees one. But now that I was back on the streets, it was time to pay the piper.

In order to keep my supply coming and pay off my debts, I had to have more money. In addition to stealing more cars, I turned to armed robbery. I never enjoyed the danger associated with armed robbery, but I needed lots of money and I needed it fast. A thirty minute robbery will net more cash than several stolen cars, and you don't have to deal with a fence or a chop shop.

I did very well for several months. I started small, robbing neighborhood grocery stores and taverns. Before long, however, I turned to more lucrative jobs. Besides, I felt bad robbing Mom and Pop operations that depended on what I was stealing for survival. I began to expand into the more affluent suburbs and outlying shopping centers.

About nine months after Maria's father had bailed me out of jail, I was cruising down a boulevard in south Philly with some friends. We needed some cash, so we decided to look for a business to rob. After circling the neighborhood several times we decided that a local jewelry store looked like a perfect location for our crime. While one guy waited in the car, two of us went into the store. My friend distracted a couple of the employees, and I stuck a pistol in the face of the guy who looked like he owned the place and demanded all of the cash.

Apparently the store had done a good business that day because the bag of cash he handed us was full of small bills. Racing from the store, we jumped into the stolen getaway car and sped away.

We usually had no trouble getting away from the scene of a crime. We always staged our robberies at a busy time and slipped away into the traffic. The police must have been very close to the store, however, because within a few minutes the rotating red lights of a police car flashed behind us.

The madness had finally reached the limit; the roller coaster ride was over. This time they had me and I wasn't getting away. Cruelly, the policemen spread-eagled us against the car and searched for weapons. Throwing our guns and what drugs we had into a pile, they jerked our arms behind us to handcuff us. Throwing us into the back seat of the two police cars that had sped to the scene, we were off to jail.

The running was finally over. All of the charges that I had accumulated under aliases and all of the times I had jumped bail were consolidated into a patchwork quilt of crime that covered any chance of escape. This time they had the goods on me. If convicted of all of the charges, I faced between fifteen and thirty years behind bars. The judge at the arraignment let me know that he expected to acquire guilty verdicts on all charges and sentence me to the fullest extent of the law.

My family had abandoned me, all of the friends I ever had were either dead, in jail, or running from the law. I was living from hand to mouth without hope. Life, for all practical purposes had come to an end.

Luis speaks at a youth Convention for young people in the Gulf Latin District of the Assemblies of God

Chapter Eleven

My Big Surprise

I was treated like someone with the plague during the time I spent in prison. My court appointed attorney spent a grand total of 15 minutes with me, just long enough to inform me that only mercy could help me now. The social rehabilitation worker assigned to my case didn't even come into the cell. Speaking with me through the bars, she informed me that I was incorrigible and that she was going to spend what little time she had with someone she might be able to help. The only visitor I had during the three weeks I spent in jail was a tall, skinny preacher by the name of Jay Cole.

Jay Cole was the director of institutional visitation for an organization called Teen Challenge. Teen Challenge was founded during the early 1960's by an Assemblies of God minister, David Wilkerson. Driven by a desire to help the troubled gang members of New York City, Wilkerson established the most successful rehabilitation program in existence. Teen Challenge is based entirely upon the life changing power of Christ. It has a success rate over nine times greater than any government run program. The work of Teen Challenge had spread to many major cities around the world, including Philadelphia.

I had absolutely no use for Jay Cole or his program. I wasn't in the best of moods anyway when the loudspeaker in the prison announced that I had a visitor. I was still suffering from the effects of cold turkey withdrawal from drugs, and my future was an absolute blur. I finally decided to go and see what idiot might waste their time coming to see someone like me.

To say I was cool to the preacher from Teen Challenge is putting it mildly. As a matter of fact, the reception I gave him was frigid. I finally agreed to allow him to pray for me just to get rid of him. His powerful prayer haunted me during the next 24 hours. It was unlike any prayer I had ever heard. It was an unsettling prayer, I had never heard anyone pray like he did. There wasn't even anyone in Uncle Frank's little storefront church who prayed like this guy prayed. Jay Cole prayed loud!

It wasn't just the volumn of the prayer that affected me though. There was a strange and mysterious magnetism that tugged at the long forgotten strings of my soul. Something about his prayer struck dread and hope into my heart at the same time. It's hard to explain, but I felt heaven's awesome presence when that tall, skinny man prayed.

My formal arraignment was to be held the very next day. When the appointed hour arrived, I was handcuffed and marched back down the corridor to face the judge. When my turn came, I was escorted into the richly paneled courtroom and placed in front of the bench.

Though this room was built for people like me, I couldn't help but feel out of place. The courtroom was beautifully ornate and decorated in expensive style. What few were present wore conservative Hart, Shaffner, and Marx suits. The blue denim prison garb I had been issued made a less than imposing presentation.

It was just another midsummer's day in court for everyone but me. Day after day they faced the likes of me. It was a very important day in my life though. The proceedings that would change my life were about to begin. I glanced about to see no one present but a couple of attorneys, the bailiff, a court reporter, and the black-robed judge. I guess a Puerto Rican punk busted on robbery charges isn't big news in Philadelphia.

"Young man," the judge glared at me over his bifocals, "you have a serious record of longstanding duration. The crimes for which you are charged are grave in nature. If convicted, you will suffer most severe consequences. Do you have anything to say for yourself before we begin?"

What could I say that would have helped anything? I simply stood with my head drooped, awaiting destiny.

After waiting several moments for my reply the judge pursed his lips and boomed, "Who's here representing Torres?"

Seeing no response, he turned to me again and said, "Young man, isn't there anyone here to help you?"

"No, sir."

"Family?"

"No."

"Friends?"

"Where's your lawyer?"

"I don't know, sir."

"Isn't there anyone?"

"No sir, no one," I replied. "No one."

It had been a long day and the judge's boiling point wasn't many degrees above his current temperature.

"For the last time!" he roared. "Is there anyone here representing Torres!"

I had heard the double doors swing open behind me a moment before and suddenly a voice rang out from the back of the courtroom.

"I'm here representing Torres," came a voice that mingled with the sound of quick steps approaching the bench.

As the bailiff hurried to stand between the judge and the sudden intrusion, I turned to see who in the world belonged to the voice. I couldn't believe my eyes! It was Jay Cole, the tall, skinny preacher from Teen Challenge!

While I stared up at him in absolute shock, the judge inquired, "And who might you be?"

"I'm Jay Cole, your honor, from Philadelphia Teen Challenge," he said as he straightened the bony frame inside the worn black suit. Shifting his big, black Bible to the other hand, he continued. "I've come requesting an audience with you as a minister of the Gospel."

Removing his glasses in an obvious gesture of amusement, the judge spoke again. "Just what is it you wish to speak with me about, Reverend?"

Intensity flashing from his eyes, Cole began, "I would like to ask the permission of the court to take custody of Luis Torres in the name of Teen Challenge."

The judge's smile turned into a frown as furrows appeared on his brow. "And just why should this court release someone with the record of young Mr. Torres to any program?"

"Your honor," Cole continued, "Teen Challenge is the most effective rehabilitation program on the face of the earth. We believe in the power of God to help troubled young men. God is the only One who can help Luis Torres. Please, your honor, give us a chance to allow the power of God to salvage this life."

Slowly, the judge began to shake his head. "Reverend, with all due respect to your God and your program, I will not release Luis Torres from the custody of this court under no circumstance. Luis Torres is an example of the lowest levels of our society."

Already, the bailiff began leading Cole from the courtroom. Our eyes joined for a brief moment as he turned to leave. All I could see was compassion.

Gathering up his papers, the judge said, "Seeing no one here to represent Torres, I call this court adjourned."

With a bang of the gavel, I was returned to the cell. Throwing myself on the bunk, I tried to collect my whirling thoughts. Who did this guy think he was? Not only did he come to see me in the hospital when I had hepatitis, he came to see me in this stinking jail. Now he shows up at my hearing. Maybe he really does care. I had at first considered this Teen Challenge thing some kind of racket. After all, in my world, nobody does anything for anybody. What was this guy's angle?

When curfew came at 10 o'clock and the lights were out, I tried to sleep, but couldn't. I was absolutely confused. My life as a free man was about to come to an end. My future was a haze. I had been abandoned by everyone. And if this was not bad enough, some guy I didn't even know was offering the power of a God I didn't want to know. As I tossed the wee hours of the night away, I didn't know daylight would present me with one of the biggest surprises of my life.

I was playing cards with several cellmates when I heard my name called over the public address system.

Oh no, I thought. It's that crazy preacher again! But when the guard met me at the bars, he told me to get my things together before I went with him. That wasn't hard; I stuck my toothbrush in my pocket and off we went.

I tried to figure out what was going on as we walked up the hallway toward the front desk. Maybe I was being transferred to another prison. Maybe I was being reassigned to solitary confinement. I hadn't done anything especially wrong while I had been here, but the judge seemed to have it in for me.

The next few minutes were a whirl of events that I haven't truly figured out to this day. At ten o'clock in the morning I was a hopelessly incarcerated young man facing 15 years in prison, maybe 30. At 10:30 I stood on the steps of the Federal Building, a free man. Apparently a coincidental clerical error resulted in a lower echelon bureaucrat mixing my case up with someone else's. Miraculously, I was released.

Needless to say, I stood on those granite steps in a daze. The sun I hadn't seen for weeks glared into my eyes as the bustling pedestrians hurried about me.

Chapter Twelve

I Need A Fix

I found myself in unbelievable circumstances as I faced freedom. I had absolutely no idea why I had been released from jail. I didn't have a dime. I was dressed in prison garb; blue denim shirt, blue denim pants, and standard issue boots. I didn't own a suit of street clothes. The clothes I had on when arrested were all the clothes I owned. They weren't fit to keep and the police threw them away.

My first thought was to get some heroin and shoot up. I had been away from the drug for three months now. My body was free, but my mind was still hooked. The demons once again clenched my mind in their unholy grip and led me back into the embrace of my killer.

I was downtown, on unfamiliar turf, so I faced a long walk to North Philly. I immediately looked up some of my old friends to bum some cash. When I walked in the door of the bar, you would have thought they had seen a ghost.

Jumping up, they shouted, "Wha' chyou doin' out, man? I didn't think we'd ever see you again!"

"I don't know what's going on," I answered. "Give me some bread so I can go see my man."

I got fifteen dollars to buy three nickel bags of dope and went directly to the pusher's house. I knocked on his door, and after what seemed like forever, he opened it just enough to see that it was me.

"Give me three nickle bags of dope, man," I shouted. "I've got to have some relief."

When he opened the door to get the stuff for me, I could see that he and his old lady had been lying on the floor getting high. When he returned, I asked him for the works to shoot up with.

Taking the snowy white powder and the works to shoot up with down the street to an abandoned tenement house, I set up shop. Quickly removing the lace from one of my shoes, I restricted the blood in the veins of my arm. I cooked the stuff and pulled it into the syringe, thrusting the needle into a vein. I expected an exhilirating rush, but nothing happened.

I lay against the wall for several minutes, waiting for the thrill, but nothing happened. The only response I got was a nauseated feeling. I had experienced some bad reactions before, but never anything like this. The only time anything close to this had happened was when I had been sold some bad stuff.

That dude burned me! I thought. I was furious. Throwing the syringe aside, I ran to a friend's apartment. He wasn't home so I broke the door in and grabbed his pistol. No pusher was going to burn me and get away with it!

I raced back to the pusher's house and up the stairs. I banged on the door with the butt of the pistol until he once again staggered to answer it. When he opened it a crack to see who was there, I shoved the pistol into his face and grabbed him by the throat. His old lady screamed, and throwing the sheet around her naked body, she ran from the room.

"You burned me, man!" I hissed through clenched teeth. "Nobody burns me and gets away with it. What d'ya think, just because I've been locked up three months, I wouldn't recognize bad stuff when you sold it to me?"

The pusher was scared out of his wits. I had the barrel of the pistol shoved so far under his chin he was looking straight up, his eyes violent with fear. I was deranged, crazed, I couldn't tolerate any more tampering with my life.

"No, you've got it wrong," he shouted. "I gave you good stuff, uncut, clean, good stuff! Turn me loose and I'll give you another bag free, you can even shoot up here. C'mon, man, I'll show you, just turn me loose and put that gun down."

Slowly I lowered him to the floor. Waving the pistol across the room, I said, "C'mon, get the stuff. I haven't got all day."

He went across the room and pulled a drawer out of a dilapidated piece of furniture, returning with another bag. I tore it open and poured a few granules of the white powder on my tongue. It was the real thing.

He helped tie a rubber hose around my upper arm and mixed the dose. I shot two cc's of madness into my veins, and the same eerie feeling spread throughout my body. No rush, no exhiliration, only an awesome feeling that something was wrong. A pain in the pit of my stomach grew more intense. Without even looking at the pusher, I staggered into the hallway, down the stairs, and into the street.

What in the world was going on? I was still totally confused as to why I had been released from jail several hours ago. My mind began to play tricks on me. I even began to imagine that the cops had released me just so they could track me down and shoot me, claiming I had escaped. As police cars drove by, I ducked into alleys. As I saw policemen on foot ahead of me, I crossed the street to avoid them. I was becoming completely paranoid.

I began to wander aimlessly through the streets. Even though Philadelphia had been my home for several years, I lost track of where I was. I was lost and confused. Besides that, I was becoming sicker by the minute.

I wandered for hours, until about 8 o'clock that night. I finally collapsed on the stoop of a building, on a busy boulevard, in the heart of the city. I lay there for some time, desperately holding my stomach in pain, wondering what would become of me.

After I sat groaning for quite some time I looked at the sign above my head. From the yellow glow of the street lamp I could make out the letters painted on it: "1620 Broad Street," and the next line, "Headquarters — Teen Challenge."

Teen Challenge! That was the program the tall, skinny preacher worked for! I couldn't believe my eyes. As far as I could remember, Jay Cole had never told me where Teen Challenge was located, only giving me his name and telephone number. I had wandered all day and half of the night, lost. In a city of five million people, with hundreds of thousands of addresses, I had crashed on the steps of the one program that had offered me any help whatsoever.

Struggling upright, I stared at the sign above my head. Teen Challenge. I had tried everything else. My life was a complete failure. No longer was there any need to hide; I had hit rock bottom with a thud and no one knew it better than I. My body was an emaciated mess, my mind a disaster. I had no future to consider. Only one person on earth had shown any interest in me whatsoever. Only Jay Cole had tried. Maybe, I thought, maybe I should give the tall, skinny preacher's God a try.

Staggering up the steps to the door, I leaned on the bell. Teen Challenge in Philadelphia was a large ministry, embracing a main downtown center, a home for boys, a home for girls, a farm, and offices. Literally dozens of volunteers worked around the clock. Out of all of the possible workers who might have answered the doorbell, who do you think swung the big door of 1620 Broad Street open? You guessed it, Jay Cole. He looked into my hopeless eyes and his face broke into a big grin.

"Why, Luis!" he cried. "Come right on in, we've been expecting you!"

Expecting me! You've got to be kidding! This guy came to see me in prison, and I did everything but spit in his face. When no one else in the world showed up to stand with me in court, he cared. But the judge informed him that it would be a long time before Luis Torres saw the light of freedom.

Through it all, he had been expecting me.

Jay Cole led me into the big hallway of the Teen Challenge Center and began introducing me to everyone in sight. As he said my name, each one shouted, "Praise the Lord!" Every person involved with Teen Challenge had been calling my name in prayer every day. I felt like I had just landed on another planet. These people weren't like anyone I had ever known. I could tell by the scars on some and by the tattoos on others that they had once lived in my world, but even they seemed to fit in here now.

He took me to the make-shift office on the first floor, and we sat down and began filling out some forms. Unable to find a pencil, he went upstairs to look for one. While he was gone, I sat slumped in the chair, eyes glazed.

I suppose I looked pretty pathetic. I had shrunk to 140 pounds. My skin was pale and motley. The whites of my eyes were yellow, and I hadn't shaved or combed my hair for days. While I was waiting for Cole to return, the director of the center, Bob Bartlett, happened to walk down the hallway. After he had passed by the door of the office, he spun around as if doing a double-take. He stood staring at me for a moment before he spoke.

"Son," he said, "walk away from God now, and you'll die on the corner of a rooftop with a needle in your arm."

Jay Cole returned and we finished the necessary paperwork. "Well, did you bring your clothes?" he asked.

I was ashamed to tell him that everything I owned in the world was on my back. I quickly decided that I could go to Nettie's house and borrow some of her husband's things.

"Naw," I said, "I need to go and pick them up. I'll be back in just a few minutes."

I walked out the door and began the long trek to her house. I didn't even have money for bus fare. As I started north along Broad Street, I felt different than when I went in. I was still the same old junkie, nothing had really changed. But I had hope. I thought maybe I really was going to get some help. I was still extremely nauseated from the drugs I had taken, but things were looking up.

I figured Nettie would be glad to see me, but the first thing she asked was how I got out of jail. I told her that I didn't know why I was out, but I needed some clothes because I was going to Teen Challenge for help. I could tell by the look in her eyes that she wanted to believe, but just couldn't. I had been down this road before.

I finally convinced her to let me have some of her husband's old clothes and ten cigarettes. I asked her for some money, but she refused.

"No way, Luis," she said. "You'll just spend it on more drugs."

I denied it, telling her that I was going to change, but she still didn't believe. She finally gave me the exact bus fare to Broad Street. I kissed her and left.

When I got off the bus at 20th and Broad Streets, I looked down the street toward the Teen Challenge Center. Those four blocks seemed like miles. For a few seconds I wrestled with my mind that was trying to talk me out of entering the program. Finally I squared my shoulders and walked toward the narrow, four-story building.

Jay Cole answered the doorbell and, with a big grin, ushered me inside. I could tell by his expression that he was surprised to see me again. To tell the truth, when I left to get some clothes, he thought that was the last he would ever see of me. I guess I was a little surprised myself. For the first time in weeks, I smiled.

Chapter Thirteen

Jesus!

I was to enter the boys' home on West Cedar Street, so Jay Cole drove me there in his little car. We drove along in awkward silence. We had absolutely nothing in common. Our worlds were light years apart. He finally tried telling me what my new home was going to be like.

"You'll really like your new roommates, Luis," he said. "They are all former drug addicts and know what you are going to be going through."

"What's the schedule like?" I asked.

"Well, you go to church a lot," he replied.

That really sounded like fun. I hadn't been to church over a couple of dozen times in my life. I was already having a few doubts.

"And," he continued, "you go to Bible study, you do your chores, you have your personal devotions daily."

"Isn't there any free time?" I asked.

"Sure, you get one-half hour before you go to sleep."

"One-half hour before you go to sleep! You've got to be kidding. I think I'd rather be in jail!"

We finally arrived at the boys' home about 10:00 that

night. The Philadelphia Teen Challenge boys' home is a stately old three-story home. It had been a beautiful home in its day and it was still a striking structure as we approached it in the moonlight. It was the type of home I had been used to burglarizing. The house was dark when we arrived, and Cole had forgotten his keys.

"I can't understand it," he said "The guys all went to church tonight, but I expected them to be home by now. They really must have had a 'HALLELUJAH breakdown!'"

"A what!" I said.

"Oh, I forgot you don't know what I'm talking about," he replied. "I just meant they really must have had a good service."

"Oh," I said. "Hallelujah Breakdown!" Whoever heard of such talk. These guys must really be weird. And I am going to live with them!

They finally showed up at about 11:30. Seventeen guys piled out of a 9 passenger van, singing at the top of their lungs and slapping each other on the back. "I'll fly away, O glory. I'll fly away. When I die, hallelujah by and by, I'll fly away."

I couldn't believe my eyes or ears. I turned to Jay Cole and, with disbelief in my eyes, said, "You mean these are the guys I'm going to have to live with!"

"Sure, Luis, you'll love 'em. C'mon."

I took one final look at this crazy bunch of fanatics, took a deep breath, and stepped out of the car. I could already tell this wasn't going to work.

By the time we entered the back door of the big house we could hear the guys in the kitchen. They were having milk and cookies for a midnight snack. I was beginning to feel uncomfortable already. These guys, weird as they were, were happy and they belonged. I was a strung-out junkie, I didn't fit in anywhere. I started to hold back in the pantry, but Jay Cole was right behind me and pushed me into the light of the kitchen. I set the tattered pillowcase that held everything I owned or had borrowed on the floor and looked at the smiling faces surrounding me.

"Hey, fellows," Jay shouted, "I want you to meet a friend of mine, Luis Torres."

No sooner were the words out of his mouth than all twenty-seven of the guys were surrounding me, shaking my hand and slapping me on the back. I noticed needle scars on several of their arms and the wrinkles of hard living lined their young brows.

"You've come to the right place man," one of them said.

"Yea," shouted another. "Jesus will set you free, brother!"

Twenty-four hours ago I was sitting in a stinking jail facing a hard time. My last experience before that had been sleeping where I could, doing drugs several times a day, drinking, shooting up, and generally doing my best to reach hell as quickly as possible. Now, every face I saw was happy and smiling. Faces that had once seethed with hate now glowed with love. Hands that had stolen, killed, and maimed now held milk and cookies!

I was introduced to several of the full-time counselors at the boys' home, men who were to change my life. Duane Henders was the director. Duane proved to be my most important influence for good. He provided the Christ-like image I needed. John Etheridge was my room supervisor. Aunt Madge, an elderly lady, provided the grandmotherly influence and taught valuable Bible studies, had already called it a day.

After one last prayer, (don't these guys ever stop praying?), everyone went to bed. I was provided bed linens and assigned to a room with John Etheridge and two other boys. They were still singing as they dressed for bed and before they jumped between the covers, each one dropped to his knees one more time for a moment of prayer. When the lights finally went out, we could hear John Etheridge softly praying, "God bless John. God bless Tony. And God, especially bless Luis. Show your love to him, God. Let him know you care. Amen."

I felt a warmth deep inside when he prayed for me. As the big, old house grew quiet, I lay silently, staring at the ceiling. I was confused, but somehow at peace. Soon, I heard three snores coming from the other bunks. I was still very sick from my reaction to the drugs. Slowly, creeping from its hiding place in my eye, a warm, salty tear slipped down my cheek and onto the pillow. I hadn't shed a tear in months.

I looked out the window toward the street light, raising myself to one elbow. I had never said a prayer in my life. I didn't know how to pray, and I wasn't completely sure there was anyone up there to listen if I did pray.

Only the snores of my roommates broke the silence of the night. Softly, barely moving my lips, I whispered, "God, if you are real, help me."

I heard nothing in reply, but I sensed some hope for a change. Maybe, just maybe, my life could be better.

I entered the program on Tuesday. The next several days were a roller coaster ride of emotion for me. For a few hours I would think that these people had the answer. Then I would decide they were all crazy and that I needed to get back to the streets. One moment I was grateful to Teen Challenge for helping me, and the next I thought they were trying to convince me of something that wasn't true.

Days at the boys' home were a continuous round of meals, chores, Bible class, rest, devotions, Bible study, and church. Then a few hours sleep and the whole process began again. Even though my body was still free from the drugs, my mind was tormented with temptation.

We attended a revival service somewhere in the Delaware valley region every night. You must remember, these people were not the reverent, churchy type that had no power. The services we attended were boisterous, powerful affairs that tended to last for several hours. Church services were punctuated with shouts of Hallelujah! and Praise the Lord! Clapping their hands and lifting their arms in the air, these happy, exuberant converts sang to the Lord with all their hearts and lungs! I spent the first few services holding back, unable to believe my eyes! I knew that I didn't have the answers, but as the week wore on, I came to the conclusion that these fellows didn't either.

I argued strongly with Duane Henders about attending the Sunday services. I wanted to stay at home while they went to their "holy-roller rally." The director finally told me I had to go if I was to stay at the center. I went, but in body only. I sullenly sat in the pew, oblivious to the service going on about me.

Looking back, I realized that the devil was trying to keep me from finding the help I needed. I was on the verge of accepting God's relentless love and Satan was making a last-ditch effort to keep his grip on me.

I didn't sleep well Monday night. The extreme nausea was still with me, and the convicting power of the Holy Spirit was dealing with my wayward heart.

As I lay in the darkness, I could hear the soft snores of the other guys in the program. I knew they loved me. As uneasy as I was, I knew their love wasn't fake, it was real. Softly wafting their way upstairs were the groaning petitions of one of the counselors. I knew he was in prayer, and I knew he would be calling my name. Though I had to admit the reality of their experience with God, my heart was struggling within me. Satan was doing his very best.

Every argument the devil could conjure up raced through my mind. "This won't work for you," he whispered. "You're not good enough for these people. God couldn't love you after all of the evil things you have done. Why don't you just go back out on the streets where you belong. You just can't make it. Luis, you're a loser."

I made my mind up as the first streaks of daylight peeked in the window. I must leave, and I must leave today.

I clearly remember that morning's breakfast. The boys who had kitchen detail brought steaming platters of hotcakes to the table. I had already seen the staff pray the food in several times during the few days I had lived in the big boys' home. The hotcakes were cold by the time we sat down to eat them, however. The young man who was asked to offer thanks for the meal must have been filled with the Holy Spirit the night before, it seemed like he would never stop.

I was quiet through breakfast. I had made my decision. I would leave. I planned to speak to Duane as soon as the dishes were washed.

Hanging my apron on a nail, I walked from the kitchen to the big walnut door to Duane's office. He let me in and I sat down before this guy I had already grown to love and told him what I had decided to do.

"Luis," he said, "you can't leave now. You are just beginning to soak up the Gospel. Give it just a few more days, man. You can't go back on the street, you know what that will mean. You'll be a dead junkie and nobody will even care that you're gone."

"I've got to go, Duane. I made up my mind last night. This Jesus stuff just isn't for me. I'm going back to the streets. I know where I belong. Duane, I've really tried. I have even prayed to ask God into my heart, and it seems I can't get through. I am really thankful that He let me stay here with you fellows for a while, but it's time for me to leave. I guess the social worker was right, I am hopeless."

I was a long way from cured, but the street-cool hoodlum I had been was being broken by the love of this bunch of Christians. Duane asked me to stay just one more night. I didn't see how just one more night could hurt, so I agreed.

Looking me right in the eye, Duane said, "Luis, God brought you here by a miracle. He didn't bring you here just to see you go back to the old life. I'm calling a prayer meeting for the rest of the day. We're going to pray that Jesus Christ saves you tonight. Luis, let's set a deadline for God. I believe that if you will give Him one more chance, and really mean it, He'll come through. If He doesn't, you'll be free to walk out that door."

I gave my word to attend one more church service. What difference could one more church service make? But, as I walked from Duane's office, something was stirring inside. I had no fear of death; I had looked death in the eye and come back. I had no fear of the law. I had no fear of the muggers or the gangs, I had grown up with those threats. But, I had heard these Teen Challenge boys pray, and I had seen the results of their prayers.

Shortly, the bell rang, signalling everyone to come to the chapel. As soon as everyone was seated, Duane stood up to speak.

"Guys, we're going to change the schedule today. Each of you is acquainted with Luis, and he has become your friend. I know you have been praying for him everyday."

Heads bobbed in agreement all over the room.

"Luis just told me that he was going to leave. I asked him to stay one more night and attend one more service, and he has agreed. I'm calling a prayer meeting for the rest of the day. I want you to pray that Luis will receive Christ into his heart at the service tonight. You know what a difference Christ has made in your own life. That's what Luis needs."

Heads were nodding even more vigorously. Within seconds, everyone was on his knees in prayer. Black guys, white guys, Hispanics, all sizes, colors and shapes were calling my name before the Lord.

As I rose to leave the room, John Etheridge, who was kneeling beside me, looked up through tear-stained eyes and said, "Luis, Jesus wants to change your life. He loves you."

I paced all day. They prayed all day. Most of them prayed right through lunch. If I hadn't respected Duane so much, I would have left right then. But, I thought too much of him to let him down now. Finally, everyone left the chapel to eat the evening meal and prepare for the evening service.

Not a one even uttered a condemning word. Their every attitude and spoken word was filled with love. I had never been around anything like the love that filled this big, old house.

Finally, all of us were piled into that old van, and we began the journey to the church in Medford, New Jersey.

Hundreds came to receive Jesus into their hearts at a
Youth convention in Texas.

Chapter Fourteen

I Found Him

The one hour van ride to the church was a typical journey. There is no happier group on earth than a vanload of former drug addicts who have found Christ. The old van almost rocked from side to side as everyone on board clapped his hands to the beat of the happy gospel tunes.

This was the first time a Teen Challenge group had visited the church in Medford. The ushers at the door probably wondered just what they were getting into as the group stepped smartly through the door, shaking hands with all of the local people, and shouting, "Well, Praise the Lord!"

The service began soon after we arrived, and within minutes the presence of the Holy Spirit was sweeping across the congregation. The power of God was so real it seemed like waves of glory rushing from one side of the sanctuary to another. The song-leader was masterfully leading the congregation in worship, smoothly switching from upbeat choruses to reverently worshipful compositions as he was led by the Holy Spirit. Teen Challenge boys love to sing and shout to the fast songs, but they are also expert at praising the Lord with the lovely worship choruses of our day. Almost every hand in that little, New Jersey church was lifted in praise as the strains of "Alleluia," a chorus born in a New York Teen Challenge prayer meeting, swept their way to heaven.

Bob Bartlett, director of Philadelphia Teen Challenge, was scheduled to preach that evening, but the presence of God was so real he simply stepped to the microphone and continued to lead in worship. Though I was definitely on everyone's mind, I was completely forgotten in the rich presence of the Lord that had permeated the service.

I experienced the strangest sensation during the next few moments. Though I was surrounded by scores of people, I felt as if I were all alone with God. I was vaguely aware of everything that was going on about me, but it was as if I were in the eye of a hurricane, untouched by the experiences taking place about me. The presence of God was not at all intimidating, in fact, I felt as though He had wrapped His big arms around me.

There was no invitation given, no call for those who wanted to accept Christ to come, but I felt a loving hand on my shoulder which encouraged me into the aisle and to the altar area at the front of the building. I thought Duane, or maybe John, Eldon Mincks, or one of the other guys from the boys' home had placed their hand on my shoulder in encouragement, but when I reached the altar, I turned around and found no one there. No doubt God's loving hand had been my guide.

I stood alone for several moments. I was not uncomfortable; I sensed a peace like I had never known before. I didn't know what to do, but somehow I knew that I was where God wanted me. Tears were flowing down my face. I didn't understand what was happening to me, but I liked it. Everyone else was so caught up in the glory of the moment that they failed to see me. All must have looked up at once, however, because suddenly, it seemed like the whole church had surrounded me.

I heard Duane's familiar voice praying behind me, and I turned to him. "Duane," I choked through the tears, "I don't know what to do."

Lovingly and wisely, he said, "Luis, just talk to God with your heart. Tell Him that you are sorry for your sins and that you want to give your heart to Him. Tell Him how you feel, Luis, He cares."

All around me were crying, praying, rejoicing boys. The noise was deafening, but I scarcely heard it as I turned around once again and began to talk to God.

I turned my tear-drenched face toward heaven and, with my eyes wide open to try to see God, I poured out my heart to Him.

"God," I began, "I know I don't deserve Your great love. My life is in a mess, my whole past is one huge disaster. I am in pain, I am a drug addict. I really don't know what's going on, but I feel Your love. God I know that I'm not much, but I want to give what's left of my life to You. Please help me God, please help me."

With that simple prayer, it was as if a dam had burst inside me. The tears had started, but now they came like a river. I couldn't stop. But the oddest thing happened. Though I was crying uncontrollably, I had a smile that stretched from ear to ear. I had never experienced such a happy feeling inside. To this day I really don't know how to describe it, but where I felt dirty before, I suddenly felt clean. It felt like I was being scrubbed on the inside, and it felt good. I had been a sinful, dirty creature for years, and I knew it. But now, all of a sudden, I felt pure and white on the inside. Jesus had come into my heart.

After several minutes, I turned around to face Duane, who had been praying directly behind me. As if on cue, every boy turned to face me, silent. I stood for a moment, face glowing, before I smilingly announced, "Duane, Jesus is in my heart! I can feel Him, He's there!"

Like a clap of thunder, everyone suddenly shouted, "Hallelujah!" Their prayers had been answered. Everyone of them had to hug me at least twice and victory was in the air. When the shouting had finally reached a dull roar, we could hear the organ playing, and all of us started singing the words of the old gospel song, *"Victory in Jesus."*

We sang for about another hour before we all piled back

in the van for the trip home. I don't think that van ever touched the pavement during the entire trip back to Philadelphia; I think it floated on the wings of angels! From daylight to dark, from life to death, my life had completely changed in a moment of time. The old Luis was gone forever, a new day had come. The old had passed away, the new had come! Life was worth living for the first time since I was a little boy.

We stood around the big kitchen as usual when we arrived home, having a midnight snack. I'm sure I looked somewhat comical, a big grin permanently plastered across my face while I shoved cookies in my mouth. It was a joyous night at the boys' home. We finally all made it to bed, John Etheridge saying his usual prayer in my room. I didn't sleep much though. I didn't stay awake from the pain in my abdomen that had bothered me since I had shot drugs last. In fact, I suddenly realized that the pain was gone. Now, I was just basking in the glow of salvation.

It was dark in the room, but from my vantage point on the top bunk it seemed that all the world was lit by a heavenly glow. I didn't know how to pray, but I finally dropped off to sleep muttering three simple words that I meant with all of my heart, "Thank You, Jesus!"

Luis speaks at Sapulpa High School in His Home Town.

Chapter Fifteen

A Changed Life

Life changed immediately. The Bible says that when Christ is received, the old things pass away and everything becomes new. That promise certainly came true in my life. The old Luis Torres was gone, I was a new man.

I slept like a baby that night. I was finally free from the terrible sickness in my stomach that had dogged me since the last time I had taken drugs.

Not only was my body free from heroin addiction, so was my mind. I had no desire for the drug. From then on, when I drove past a group of junkies on a street corner, I had pity for them instead of envy. I was free.!

The next morning John came to wake me and simply whispered in my ear, and I shot straight up in bed, shouting, "Praise the Lord!" Jesus had saved me, and I wanted the whole world to know.

I raced down the ornate, walnut staircase from my bedroom on the third floor to the kitchen. My face must have shone like Moses, because when I hit the bottom landing, the whole gang howled with happy laughter. I literally glowed! Even those guys who were getting on my nerves looked good.

the cooks brought the steaming platters of
ast into the dining room, Duane looked around the
for someone to pray. When his eyes met mine, he
ghed. "I know better than to ask you to pray, Luis. Your
prayer would be so long the food would get cold!" I
laughed louder than anyone.

As the days went by, the joy of being saved increased
instead of growing dim. The Bible took on a new meaning.
I couldn't get enough of its precious truth. Instead of
dreading the times of Bible study and prayer, I looked
forward to them as the highlight of every day. Aunt Madge
was constantly assigning scriptures to memorize, and I
began memorizing them one after another. The Holy Spirit
had healed my mind.

The Bible became my closest friend and companion. I
spent every free moment mesmerized by its pages. The
truth of the Word of God grabbed my attention, and I was
transfixed by its powerful message. My desire to know its
truth was insatiable. I almost drove Duane and Eldon
crazy with questions about the Bible.

I always had a reasonably sharp mind, but the years of
drug addiction had taken their toll. My intelligence had not
been affected, but my ability to concentrate and use my
memory had been altered by the tremendous abuse I had
inflicted upon my brain. When I was saved, God not only
healed my soul, He put my ability to concentrate and
achieve mental mastery back in order. Boy! If the guys at
old P.S. 24 could only see me now!

God saved all of me. My body, which had become
emaciated, responded quickly to the exercise and
nutritious meals of the boys' home. My skin regained its
natural glow and my hair began to shine once again. I put
weight back on my skinny frame, and soon I was the
picture of health; divine health.

Though my life had been made complete by God's great
love, I began to realize that something was missing. I
heard the men who came to preach in chapel talk about the
baptism in the Holy Spirit. I knew I had not received this
experience, and if God had something more for me, I sure
wanted all of it.

Teen Challenge is the most successful drug rehabilitation program for young men and women in existence today. The difference between Teen Challenge and other programs is clear. Many other religious rehabilitation programs are doing a good job, but their success rate doesn't come close to Teen Challenge's. The difference is the power of the Holy Spirit. David Wilkerson was the first to put it all together when he founded Teen Challenge.

Drug addiction is the strongest stranglehold the devil can put on a human. It's more than just a chemical addiction, too. A spirit of the enemy invades the innermost being when a junkie plunges the needle into his arm. Drug addiction is a death grip on a man's soul.

The only sure cure for drug addiction is allowing the saving grace of Christ to cleanse all traces of the devil's destruction from a junkie's life and then invite the Holy Spirit to move in on a permanent basis.

As wonderful as my newfound salvation was, I still found myself troubled by doubts from time to time. As I rode in the overcrowded van to the nightly church services, I would hear a voice whisper in my ear, "You're not going to be in this religious thing forever you know. Give it up now, get a head start on life." The voice would tell me that I didn't have to go back on drugs, but deep inside I would. I was rapidly becoming a prisoner of my freedom. I knew that I couldn't stay at the Teen Challenge Center forever, and I knew that when I left, I would not have the strength to stay clean. I decided that I had to have the Baptism in the Holy Spirit so I could make it.

We attended a Sunday morning service at Highway Tabernacle in downtown Philadelphia seven weeks after I was saved. I was very tired, and Pastor Robertson's message just wasn't getting through. My head was nodding up and down as I valiantly struggled to keep my eyes open. Sunday dinner was a special time at Teen Challenge. Once a week the Italian members of the staff cooked a huge spaghetti dinner and we all feasted together. During the week we all ate in our separate home, the girls at the girls' home, the boys at our big house and the rest of the staff with their families. But noon Sunday was a giant feast with the whole Teen Challenge family invited. I just hoped to stay awake long enough to get to the spaghetti.

Although the other members of the congregation filed out of the building following the last amen, we Teen Challenge boys made our way to the altars for a time of prayer. We had been trained to close every service by spending at least a few moments in prayer.

I knew it wouldn't be right to fall asleep while praying, so I knelt behind the big pipe organ, thinking that its loudness might keep me from sleep. The pastor had not preached about the baptism in the Holy Spirit, and I was not seeking the experience, but all of a sudden I heard John Etheridge praying with all his heart that I would receive.

John had felt impressed by the Holy Spirit to kneel behind me and to begin to encourage me. That was the last thing I wanted. I knew that John was sincere, and I really did want to receive the experience, but not now, thank you. My body was weary and spaghetti was calling.

My eyes were closed, and in a few moments, John's voice was still and I heard him rising from his knees. Good, I thought, he's giving up. But, just as I began to rise from my makeshift altar behind the organ, I heard John praying directly in front of me. Not only that, I heard the prayers of several of my friends who had gathered around me to help "pray me through."

Suddenly, the sweet presence of God surrounded me, and I was filled with a great desire to have more of Him in my life. I lifted my hands high into the air and began to voice my praises as big tears of joy flowed down my cheeks. Gradually, the voices of those who were praying with me faded away, and I was lost in the marvelous presence of the Almighty.

The next sound I heard was that of my own voice. Beautiful languages I had never heard before began forming in my mouth, and I opened it wide and let them flow. Cascading from my mouth, the lovely sounds were straight from heaven. I was speaking in tongues, a language of the angels. The sounds making their way up my throat were more than just gibberish, they were well-defined and in easily recognizable syntax. For the first time in my young Christian life, I felt that I was praising God in a way truly worthy of His greatness.

But, the most awesome quality of the experience wasn't the heavenly language I found myself speaking. The words flowing from my mouth were like the breaking of a dam and, suddenly, a dynamic power roared into my soul. I was lost in a torrent of love, deliriously adrift in a tidal wave of the Holy Spirit.

After an hour and a half that seemed like a split second, I once again became aware of those about me. I tentatively opened one eye, not even sure that I was still tied to earth. I was surrounded by the entire population of the boys' home, and they were grinning from ear to ear. I stood awkwardly for a moment, suddenly feeling out of place. I had been in heavenly places, and this world was no longer my home. Finally, I began to laugh a holy laugh that came from deep down in my soul, and old Highway Tabernacle resounded with the ecstasy of thirty young men lost in the Spirit of God.

We missed the spaghetti dinner, but we didn't care; we were feasting on manna from heaven. Once again, that old van rocked its way back through Germantown to the boys' home to the beat of "By My Spirit Saith the Lord." We stood around the big kitchen in the old mansion and ate peanut butter and jelly sandwiches, grape jelly smeared across our silly grins.

I remember going to bed that night and lying awake until the wee hours of the morning, basking in the warm glow of God's radiant power. I wondered for a moment if I was still filled with the Holy Spirit, so I closed my eyes and once again that heavenly language poured from me like the whispers of a brook.

The Holy Spirit became my constant companion. The power I had felt lacking came in great proportions as I opened more of my life to the Spirit's power. The words of the Bible leaped off the page. When I came to a difficult passage, I would ask the Holy Spirit to help me. As I sat and meditated upon the problematic passage, the Spirit would bring the interpretation to me and I would find comfort.

I felt the urge to preach from the moment I was saved, but after being filled with the Holy Spirit, the urge became a call. I knew that my life was to be spent helping others find Jesus Christ.

Knowing God and His Word became an obsession. Supernaturally, my intellectual capacities had increased many times over. Six months before, when I was strung out on drugs, I had trouble understanding a comic book, but now I could grasp delicate theological principles. Duane gave me a key to his study, and I voraciously devoured his commentaries and sermon books. I was able to gain a quick understanding of the Bible because I had become well acquainted with its Author.

I burned inside with a desire to tell the world what God had done for me. Every day the weather allowed, we were out in the streets and parks, preaching the gospel. We parked an old flat bed truck in strategic spots and set up our portable public-address equipment. One of the guys who could play an instrument would begin blowing a catchy gospel tune, or our boys' home choir would sing. In a few minutes we had a congregation.

Our street services usually started with a few songs to catch their attention and then one of the converts would give his testimony. Then one of the more mature staff members would bring a short sermon, closing with an invitation to accept Christ as Saviour. I delivered my testimony so fervently and my interest in lost souls was so apparent that the staff began using me in every street meeting. As I proved my stability, they even began allowing me to take a team into the ghettoes on my own to share the gospel.

My evangelistic zeal almost became obnoxious at times. According to my roommates, I even preached in my sleep! They told me several times that I bolted to my feet and

112

preached a fiery message from the middle of my bed. Obviously, I was consumed with a desire to communicate the joy I had discovered.

Teen Challenge had received an invitation from Louisville, Kentucky, to come and conduct a short evangelistic meeting, and Duane was designated to lead the group. We loaded the van and headed south. This was to be my first trip out of the New York-Philadelphia area, so I was very excited.

Evangel Tabernacle, our destination, was a powerful church on the move. Waymon Rogers, the pastor, is a dynamic man of God. From the moment I met him, I could feel the presence of the Holy Spirit in his life. I was just a skinny Puerto Rican kid from Philadelphia, however, so I decided to just sit back and enjoy the great services we were having.

Our short crusade was only scheduled to last through the week, so when Friday evening's service closed, we began loading the equipment. I had only given a short testimony one of the nights. Bob Bartlett had been the main speaker, doing a tremendous job.

Out of the corner of my eye, I noticed Pastor Rogers and Bob Bartlett talking and looking in my direction. Brother Bartlett called me to them and said that Pastor Rogers had something to ask me. What he had to say nearly floored me.

"Luis," he began, "I noticed something special when you gave your testimony the other evening. I can tell that God has really done a work in your life."

I thanked him for his kind words and he continued. "Luis, there are a lot of troubled people out there that need Jesus. You can tell them better than I, you've been there and back. I've cleared this with your director, and I've got a proposition for you. How about staying over and preaching in our Sunday evening service. We'll pay all of your expenses back to Philadelphia next week."

I couldn't believe my ears! I was being invited to preach. And not only was I being invited to preach, I was being invited to preach in one of the most exciting churches in

America. Would I stay over? You'd better believe I would!

I nearly floated out of the building to the home where I was staying. But within an hour or so, the reality of what I was going to do hit me. I had delivered my testimony dozens of times, but I had never really preached before a live congregation of people. There's a lot of difference between preaching from your bed in the middle of the night and preaching in front of hundreds of people!

I knelt beside the bed that night and began to ask God for help. Within a few minutes I felt His calm assurance sweep over me and I knew that everything would be all right.

I prayed all day Saturday that God would give me the right message. When Sunday morning came, I was invited to sit on the platform with Pastor Rogers and the rest of the staff. I was very impressed by the compassion that flowed from these men during the service. These men of God were really dedicated to meeting the needs of the congregation. I felt their strong desire to be used of God as they worked among those who came for prayer following the sermon.

When it came time for the Sunday evening service, Pastor Rogers compassionately took me aside and told me that he had complete confidence in my ability to do a good job. He encouraged me to be very sensitive to the leading of the Holy Spirit and to follow the Spirit's directives, but that if I needed his help, he would be right behind me.

Of course, I was very nervous. I must confess that I did not receive very much edification from the song service; I was too busy trying to keep my knees from knocking! My simple, yet totally fervent, prayer in those moments was "God, please use me. Hide me behind the cross and let me help someone see the light."

When it came time for the preaching, Pastor Rogers introduced me, and I nervously stood before that great crowd of people. But when I announced the scripture text and began to speak, I felt the anointing of God fall upon me, and I spoke with authority and love. At the end of my short message, I made a very simple appeal for those who wanted to find Christ to come to the front for prayer. As the orchestra began to play, I lowered my head to pray. I was afraid to look up to see if anyone was responding, but as I lifted my tear-filled eyes, I saw that the aisles were filled with those who were coming for prayer. Not knowing what to do, I felt Pastor Rogers link his arm with mine as he said, "Come on, son, let's go pray with the people."

As we moved among those who were seeking God, my heart was warmed by the healing being done by the grace of God. I finally stepped off to one side to view what God was doing. As joy filled my soul, I lifted my hands in the air and gave God all the glory for His great love. I would never be the same; I had found my mission. My life would be spent spreading the wonderful news of God's great love.

Some Teens ask Luis Questions after a High School Assembly

Luis and Gail are welcomed at the Teen Challenge Center in Sao Paulo, Brazil

Chapter Sixteen

Free At Last

I was greeted like a hero returning from war when I returned to Philadelphia from Louisville. Everyone wanted to know how my first sermon went. While it was obvious my ministry needed more polish, I was happy to tell them that the Lord had blessed my efforts.

From that time on, I saw my life through different eyes. I was no longer in control of my future, I had sold out to God, He was now the boss. I determined to do everything possible to prepare myself to become a good servant for Him.

Within a few weeks, I had proven my trustworthiness enough to be promoted to the Junior Staff of the Teen Challenge program. I was grateful for any opportunity to serve God. I began to counsel and encourage many of the guys that were coming off the streets and into the program. I could relate to their needs; I had been there, and I knew how much an encouraging word could mean to their shaky resolves.

About that time, I was asked to accompany a young man to Puerto Rico. Even though he was young, he had become heavily involved with the Mafia, and they had determined to kill him for turning his back on the organization. He had received Christ as his Saviour and had kicked the drugs, but it wasn't safe for him to remain in Philadelphia. He and I went to Puerto Rico for several weeks and stayed with some of his relatives, waiting for the heat to blow over.

I know that my troubled years were a disappointment to my Grandfather in Ponce, and I would have wanted to tell him about what Christ had done in my life, but by this time he had died. I enjoyed seeing other members of my family, however, and was able to share the love of God with them. Willie just couldn't believe his eyes. The last time he had seen his little brother was as a junkie in trouble with the law. Now, standing before him, was a healthy, happy, clean Christian.

When I returned to Philadelphia, my family began coming to see me at the boys' home on a regular basis. When I had been at my lowest point of drug addiction, they did not come to see me because of the pain it brought to their hearts. When I first entered the program, they did not come because they were afraid the change in my life wasn't for real. Now, they felt uncomfortable coming to see me because they knew that they also needed what I had found. Finally, however, led by Alma, they began visiting me every Sunday afternoon in the parlor of the big boys' home.

Those afternoons were joyous celebrations. Nettie's children, who I hardly knew, were growing up and would run to their Uncle Luis, giggling with delight. Happily chattering in Spanish, we all rejoiced because of my newfound joy. When I tried to tell them that they needed Jesus as well, they just grew silent and hung their heads. They were very happy for me though.

I'll never forget the first time my family came to hear me give my testimony. Lined up like magpies on a telephone line, dressed in their finest clothes, the Torres family was a very proud group as they listened to the prodigal tell how Christ had brought him home. I nervously saw them dry their tears and hug each other, but while I hopefully watched their response during the invitation, they didn't respond. I determined to continue to pray that my family would also find the joy that comes with knowing Jesus.

My mother is an outstanding cook, and I craved a big helping of her delicious beans and rice. When I mentioned this to Duane and Eldon, they agreed that such cooking would do me good, but they would have to come along. I didn't mind, and after the first visit, they decided I should return there often. They loved Mom's cooking just as much as I did.

Duane finally decided that I was strong enough to visit my family alone, so he dropped me off at Alma's house. Alma had so much confidence in my new experience with God that she loaned her car to me. I drove across town to visit Mom that afternoon and had just finished eating one of her delicious meals. I was sitting outside on the stoop in the evening dusk, and a familiar form came down the street toward me. As she drew closer, I recognized the long, blonde hair; it was Mary.

She ran excitedly toward me saying, "Hey, Luis, it's good to see you! How are you doing? I haven't seen you in a long, long time. I've missed being with you."

I was excited to see her. She and I had been very close, and I immediately wanted to witness to her about what Christ had done in my life. She was also happy to see me, and we took a walk to renew acquaintances.

"You look really good, man," she said. "What has happened to you? You look so clean . . . and you've gained a little weight. You really look terrific."

As we walked together remembering old times, I could tell that she was surprised at the change she saw in me.

I shared with her how drugs were no longer a part of my life. I told her how Christ had come, made me clean and taken away any desire for the old life. I told her that He could change her too. As we wound our way through the children playing on the sidewalk, I could see a tear welling up in the corner of her eye.

Mary was still a striking girl, with her long blonde hair and pretty features, but I could see that her wayward life was catching up with her. Her small frame was growing even skinnier under her skimpy cotton blouse, and her skin had lost its lustre. She was doing a lot of methadrine, and heavy black bags hung under her eyes.

She knew she needed help, and my story of success with Jesus was hitting home. Within a few moments, however, the weak moment had passed and she was her old self. We walked on through the old neighborhood, taking in the familiar sights and sounds.

As we walked, the old ways began ingratiating themselves to me once again. When we would see one of my old buddies, they would shout a greeting and rush across the street to embrace me. It felt good to be with some of my old friends, and when Mary linked her arm through mine, I felt like I had returned home. We finally stopped and took a seat on the bench in the park, savoring the soft breeze of a mild summer night.

Turning to me, Mary spoke softly. "Luis, I've missed you. Stay with me tonight."

The enemy was really working on my mind as I began to remember the times we had been together. The sights, sounds, smells; the entire atmosphere of my home turf were working on me. I hadn't been with a woman for almost a year, and lust was about to consume me. Thoughts raced through my mind.

Satan whispered in my ear, "You can get by with this. No one will know. You've been good for months now, you deserve a little fun, reward yourself." I sat silently for several confused moments until the Holy Spirit's power began welling up inside of me.

"No, Mary," I said softly. "I can't come back. I've sold out to God and I can't turn back now."

Without speaking, we rose as one from the bench and started back to Mom's house. Some teenagers were goofing on the corner, and a boy was bouncing a rubber ball against the wall. I was sad in a way, but I knew the price had to be paid.

120

I looked into Mary's sad eyes and said goodby, got into Alma's car, and drove back to Germantown.

As I drove along, I realized what a victory I had just won. Satan had thrown his best shot at me and I withstood the blow. The Holy Spirit brought to my rememberance what the Bible says in Proverbs 7:21-24, *"With persuasive words she led him astray. She seduced him with her smooth talk. All at once he followed her, like an ox going to the slaughter, like a deer stepping into a noose 'til an arrow pierces his liver, like a bird darting into a snare, little knowing it will cost him his life. Now listen my sons, listen to me; pay attention to what I say. Do not let your heart turn to her ways or stray into her paths. Many are the victims she has brought down; her slain are a mighty throng. Her house is a highway to the grave, leading down to the chambers of death."*

When I walked in the door of the boys' home, the big house was silent. It was late, much later than I had told Duane it would be when I returned. As I walked through the kitchen, I could see light peeking out from under Duane's office door. I softly pushed it open and walked in to face him. He had been waiting for me, worried.

"How are you doing, Luis?" he said.

"I'm fine, Duane," I answered.

"Do you want to talk about it?"

He had sensed what I was going through and had been in prayer for me for the last two hours. The extent of his compassion and love for me touched me deeply. I thought of Jesus's words to Peter, *"I have prayed for you that your faith may not fail."* (Luke 22:32)

For an hour, I shared my feelings with him while he listened. Finally, he said, "Luis, I'm proud of you. You have just passed a big test." We had prayer and I left his office, knowing that Christ surely lived in me.

Several days later, I was doing my chores, whistling a gospel tune, when Duane called me into his office. He asked if I intended to serve God to the best of my ability. I said, of course, so he responded that it was time to take care of some unfinished business. It was time to go and see the judge about all of the charges that remained against me.

"You've got to be kidding!" I gasped. "Now that I've got my act together and want to begin a career as a minister, you want me to go back and confess to all of those crimes? They'll put me away so long that I'll never see daylight! No way man!" Calmly Duane encouraged me to think about it.

The thought tormented me for several days. Finally, after much prayer, I decided that I had to do the right thing and told Duane I was ready. I asked him if we were going to hire an attorney, and he told me we were going to use the finest attorney available, the power of God. We knelt and prayed that God would give me favor in the eyes of the judge. I closed Duane's prayer for him, "God, if you have ever come through, come through for me now."

The day of my appointment with the judge dawned bright and Duane and I headed downtown in the van, both dressed in our finest clothes. We knew we were taking a tremendous risk.

We waited in the airy courtroom through the several cases scheduled before us. I sat amazed at the scenario in front of me. The troubled young men standing before the judge were me just twelve short months ago. I silently thanked God that a tall, skinny preacher took the time to plead my case the last time I was here.

The docket was lengthy that day and the judge was clearly tired and exasperated when it came my turn. The bailiff announced my name and I stood before the judge.

"Son," the judge peered over his glasses at me, "your case is most unusual. According to your record here, you are a most troublesome young man. But, you don't look like a hoodlum and they tell me you no longer act like one. Would you mind telling me your story?"

I'm sure he didn't realize what he was getting himself into. I was getting rather accustomed to giving my testimony, and I began at the beginning, just as if I was in church. He would usually have stopped such a long-winded discourse, but he continued to listen, spellbound.

Thirty minutes later, I finished my speech, complete with a blow-by-blow account of the day I was saved and how God filled me with the Holy Spirit. By now, the bailiff had taken a seat in rapt attention and the court stenographer almost stopped clicking the keys in fascination. The judge sat in the exact same position he had held when I began. As I finished, he leaned back in his big leather chair, lips pursed, peering over his glasses at me. I turned to look at Duane and he simply snickered and looked at the table.

Clearing his throat, the Judge said, "Mr. Torres, your story is most amazing. In fact, I've never heard anything quite like it. I'm releasing you to the recognizance of this program and will take the case under advisement."

As we walked from the Federal Building, I was as nervous as a cat. I knew I had done the right thing, but now I had to await the verdict. For the next few days, all of the fellows of the boys' home and I spent much time in prayer that God would have His way with my case.

Finally, we received the call that the judge had reached a decision. Duane and I returned to the courtroom. As we watched, two of my old buddies were sentenced to stiff terms for lesser crimes than mine.

I nervously turned to Duane and said, "I don't think even God can get me out of this. Are you sure we have done the right thing. The judge is in a real bad mood today."

Duane looked at me in confidence, "God will honor you for telling the truth, Luis. Let's just leave it in His hands."

I sure hope so, I thought. It isn't Duane facing prison, it is me.

"Luis Torres," the bailiff announced, "approach the bench." I stood meekly before the judge, realizing my whole life hung in the balance.

The judge cleared his throat and said, "Luis, for the last ten days, I have examined your case from top to bottom. I find that it warrants a stiff prison sentence. I have also sent a caseworker to your old neighborhood to validate your story. He reported to me that your friends substantiate your story. They have seen you on the street corners telling others about the change in your life."

"Therefore, the court has reached the decision to drop all charges against you so you can go help others."

With a bang of the gavel, he said, "Case dismisssed," and I was free. With tears in his eyes, Duane jumped from his seat and shouted, "Praise the Lord!" We walked from the court room and hugged on the steps of the Federal Building. I walked out the door of the Federal Building with a clear record. I looked at Duane and cried, "Duane, I am free, I am free. Jesus has set me free. I can't believe it. He has really set me free!"

**"HE WHOM THE SON SETS FREE
IS FREE INDEED."**

Luis and Gail Minister in Gatesvile Texas at a Womens Prison

Epilogue

A thick fog surrounded Philadelphia as the big jet zoomed up and westward. In minutes we were above the clouds, speeding to Tulsa, Oklahoma. I had spent several days in the New York-Philadelphia area visiting family and refreshing my memory to write this book. It has now been several years since the judge cleared all charges against my name. As the stewardess served beverages to those around me, I reclined and reminisced.

It seems like just yesterday that I left Teen Challenge to attend Bible school in the midwest. While there I received many opportunities to preach and began my ministry. One of those preaching opportunities took me to the little town of Fairfax, Oklahoma. On the fifth row of that little church sat the most beautiful young lady I had ever laid eyes on. Though I didn't speak to her that night, I could tell by the look in her eyes that sparks were exploding between us.

Following the service, as casually as possible, I asked the pastor the name of the pretty girl. With a knowing twinkle in his eye, he told me her name was Gail Morris, and that she was practically engaged to a local boy. I tried to put her out of my mind, but those dark eyes just kept smiling at me.

The Holy Spirit spoke to my heart that she was to be my wife. On our second date, I proposed. Now we travel around the world sharing the Good News. We have been blessed with a handsome son Mark, who will never have to wonder if he is loved.

"Mr. Torres, do you care for more coffee?" asked the stewardess. I had been locked in my daydreams as I thought of the good things God has done for me. I thank God every day for delivering me from the hell that was my destiny, but seeing the old memories face to face reminded me how miraculous the story really was.

I had returned to Tinton Avenue, where I played as a boy. The whole block had been levelled. The residents had finally destroyed the buildings. The school Willie and I attended still stands but is just an abandoned shell, its windows broken and gaping open to swallow the filth of the city. Nothing was the same so I bought a bottle of soda pop at the corner market where we used to steal and drove to where Papi and Luisa live today.

They still live in the same part of town and work for the same company. I always enjoy seeing Papi. We sit together on the stoop when I come. We still don't have a lot to say, but the silence is peaceful now. Papi is happy that I found Christ, but though I have encouraged him to receive Him, he never changes. I pray he will find the Lord.

I spent most of the visit in Philadelphia. Most of my memories are from there, and Mom and my brothers and sisters live there. Mom and Nettie only live a few doors apart and when I go to see them, it seems like I have stepped back into my teenage years. Children still play in the narrow streets between the abandoned cars and hollow-eyed boys and girls still goof off on the corner. As I walked up the sidewalk to Nettie's house, I had to go around a car where a young Puerto Rican sat listening to deafening Spanish music, drug-filled head bobbing to the beat.

Maybe the best part of coming home is when we all

gather to enjoy Mom's good cooking. As we fill our plates with rice, hot sausages, and savory meats, we talk about our families. Willie is married and has a family now. Alma is still a nurse and has two children. Nettie and her family are the hosts and we have such a good time together.

While there, I rented a car and made the three hour drive to the small town in northern Pennsylvania where Jay Cole pastors. I enjoyed Sunday dinner with him and his lovely family. He is still just as tall and skinny as ever, and he is still reaching lost souls.

The old boys' home is still filled with young men of all colors. Each has found Christ and is making a new life by the power of the Holy Spirit. I didn't stay long, the faces have all changed. Duane Henders is now a missionary in Portugal, and the others have found other posts of duty as well. But the stately old mansion is still giving birth to new lives.

Perhaps the saddest part of the trip was a visit to my old neighborhood. I parked my car down the block and walked the rest of the way. I was still quite a ways away when I heard someone shout, "Hey, Anthony!" Before I got there, they had run to greet me.

While there, I ran into Pedro Juan. We went into his house and visited almost all afternoon. For quite a while we joked and laughed, but when I started asking about some of the old friends, he began to look depressed. One by one he listed them, some in jail, some still wandering the streets, and a few dead, either murdered or dead of an overdose. When I told him about Christ, tears filled his eyes. I pray Pedro Juan finds Him.

Now, however, it was time to leave. As the jet swept me back to my home in Oklahoma, I counted my many blessings. The story doesn't end here, it only begins. Every year I crisscross America, preaching in churches, schools, conventions, and prisons. In each instance I share with them the love of Christ and the truth that He can change their lives just like He changed mine.

I am often allowed to share my story in high schools and in prisons. It never fails, following such a presentation,

127

aimless people headed down the same road I trod find their way to me, looking for hope.

No one could be born more hopeless than I was. As I grew up, my hopelessness just became worse instead of becoming better. When I stood before the judge after being arrested for the jewelry store robbery, I had reached the absolute end of the line. I was DESTINED FOR HELL! That I was given another chance and miraculously found Christ shows the extent of God's great love.

Perhaps you are in need of Christ as well. For years I hopelessly hoped that life would get better. Christ became that hope. Today He is my reality. He can be yours as well. The same Love that reached down to me is reaching out to you today. Receive it!

The Torres Family, Luis, Gail, Jeff, Mark and Christal